The Islanders

Also by John Rowe Townsend

The Invaders
King Creature Come
The Xanadu Manuscript
Noah's Castle
Top of the World
Forest of the Night
The Summer People
Goodnight, Prof., Love
The Intruder
Pirate's Island

John Rowe Townsend

The Islanders

Oxford University Press

Oxford Toronto Melbourne

Oxford University Press, Walton Street, Oxford OX2 6DP

Oxford New York Toronto
Delhi Bombay Calcutta Madras Karachi
Petaling Jaya Singapore Hong Kong Tokyo
Nairobi Dar es Salaam Cape Town
Melbourne Auckland

and associated companies in
Berlin Ibadan

Oxford is a trade mark of Oxford University Press

A CIP catalogue record for this book is available
from the British Library

Printed in Great Britain by
Billing & Sons Ltd, Worcester

For Leon and Vivien

AUTHOR'S NOTE

The history and geography of my island of Halcyon owe a good deal to those of Pitcairn Island in the Pacific Ocean and Tristan da Cunha in the South Atlantic. But the people of Halcyon, and their beliefs and attitudes, are entirely imaginary.

J.R.T.

First Wave

THE *island is a tiny dot in a vast expanse of ocean. Its name is Halcyon. You would find it hard to get there, for it has neither harbour nor airstrip, and ships steer clear of its dangerous reefs. No travel agency will offer you a ticket. But there is no harm in imagining a visit. You might, if you had plenty of money and knew your way around, get a passage on a tramp steamer with a cooperative captain. The weather might be mild by Halcyon standards, though fierce by any others; an island boat might pluck you perilously from the ship's side and swirl you past rocks and reefs to the little inlet that serves as a landing-place. You would be soaked with spray, and thankful to be safely ashore.*

Having landed on Halcyon, you would scramble up a steep dirt track and find yourself on a green treeless upland, edged with sheer cliffs and dominated by the steep cone of a sleeping volcano. Behind and before you would be a seascape of rolling saltwater hill and valley: a massively-moving sea, endlessly breaking to pieces against the black volcanic coast and foaming around jagged rocks. The winds that blew around you might come, according to season, cold from the Antarctic, warm from the Equator, or rainbearing from a thousand miles of ocean to east or west. Fifteen miles away, if you looked toward the sunset on a clear day, you might see the companion island of Kingfisher, a small dark hump on the horizon.

In a hollow, sheltered from the worst of Halcyon's gales, you would find the village, with its hundred hardy souls: a last outpost of humanity, surviving precariously on a speck of land as remote and lonely in its southern seas as a planet in space. And on an early spring day, at a time now gone but not so very long ago, you might have found a girl called Molly and a boy called Thomas, sister and brother.

Chapter 1

MOLLY saw the sail first. Molly was on top of Sammy's Cliff, dreaming of driftwood. She dreamed of it not for herself but for her elder sister Beth. Great beams of oak she dreamed, fifty feet long; unsplintered spars and planks, floating ashore from a wreck far out, with nobody drowned and the sailors all saved by another ship. Wood, so that Adam could build a house for Beth and they could marry. And wood enough for a boat, to help with the fishing. Wood for two boats, perhaps . . . but no, that was going too far. Wood for a house and two boats was beyond the reach of her dreaming.

Near by was Thomas, picking wild celery among the long wet grass. Behind them both was the Peak, rearing stark in the air, circled by cloud. Round to their right, on the next face of the cliff, were the other two: thickset, sturdy Dan Wilde and small, reckless Jemmy Kane. Stepping surefooted from ledge to ledge, they were stealing the eggs of the screaming seabirds.

Sammy's Cliff was where old Sammy Oakes had fallen to his death, three generations ago. John Goodall had fallen there, too, and Emily Jonas, who was only a young girl. And others would fall in their time, everyone knew. It was a dangerous place. But birds and their eggs were food, and risks must be taken if islanders were to eat. Dan and Jemmy were not worrying; they had no fears. It was Thomas who feared the dizzying drop to the wrinkled, crawling sea below; to the sharp black rocks and reefs. It was Molly who feared for Thomas, because he hated to climb.

And it was Molly who saw the sail. It was tiny, tiny at first, and brown, and not much more than a dot on the curved horizon. She thought for a moment it was driftwood, an answer to dream and prayer. But it was coming in fast on the wind, and standing up from the sea's dark sullen surface. In a minute she was sure, and called Thomas over.

'She's running,' he said, his hand shading his eyes. 'I never seen a boat like that before.' And, a moment later, 'She'll be on the reef before long.'

They looked at each other: strong, sturdy Molly, who had wide dark eyes, a beaky nose, big mouth and almost-black hair; Thomas, like her in feature but thinner and narrower-faced. Thomas knew what Molly was thinking, but was determined.

'We better go down,' he said.

'We could shout to the others,' Molly suggested. 'They're halfway there already.' But she knew that the din of indignant seabirds wouldn't let Dan and Jemmy hear each other, never mind herself and Thomas.

'They haven't seen it,' Thomas said.

'They might, any minute,' said Molly. She was at the edge, leaning into the wind. She could see the other two, pressed tight against the cliff, moving with practised wariness, absorbed in their task, each with a shoulder-slung bag for the plundered eggs.

'Can't count on them seeing,' said Thomas. 'And they can't hurry, carrying the eggs. Come on.'

He and Molly ran along the cliff top to the point where there was a way down. Thomas went first, as was his duty, being older by a year, and the boy. Molly followed, half fearful for him, half impatient with his slowness. He moved cautiously, clinging to grassy tuft or projecting rock where she'd have taken a chance and relied on the grip of her bare feet. She could see the sweat on his forehead, though the day wasn't warm. It was hard, being an island boy and fearing heights: as hard as fearing the sea, and just as useless. Cliffs and sea were island life.

Held back by Thomas's caution, Molly pressed herself into the cliff and looked down. The sail was much farther in now. She could see the boat clearly: a light, high-sided canoe with an outrigger, not like an island craft at all. It didn't look as if there was anyone in control. The sail had been lashed into place; it was badly torn, but it was enough to move the boat swiftly in this wind. The whole thing looked desperately frail, and if it wasn't swamped by the surf it would soon hit a rock or reef. Why didn't they drop the sail, why didn't someone steer? Not that they had much chance, whatever they did. Molly's lips moved in the prayer to the Deliverer for sea saving, and then again in prayer for herself and Thomas, here on the cliff.

They were moving down a little faster now. Thomas grew bolder as he neared the cliff foot. Once he managed to grin to Molly from below; once he looked out toward the boat and grimaced. Dan and young Jemmy were far above them now, and there was still no sign that they had noticed anything amiss.

Thomas reached the bottom and ran across the narrow beach of black glistening sand. He threw off his sheepskin jacket and rough woven breeches, displaying the grey woollens he wore underneath. Then he plunged into the quiet water at the landward side of the reef, and swam out. Molly took off her jacket too, but modesty forbade any further undressing. She clambered out along the row of sharp slippery rocks that curved like a claw round the tiny bay.

The boat was on the reef now. With a thousand miles of ocean swell behind it, it rode in, bounced back, and rode in again. Its occupants weren't making any attempt to save themselves.

'Drop your sail!' Thomas called. But he couldn't hear his own voice above the roar of the surf. Molly approached from the other side of the boat, crawling perilously toward it. The boat struck the reef for the fourth or fifth time, and bounced back once more.

'Where are you?' Thomas yelled to the unseen occupants. He couldn't see over the canoe's high side. Light as it was, it would hurt if it struck him. Or Molly. At the least it would knock her, clothed, into the water.

The boat came dancing in again. Thomas grabbed the float

of the outrigger, but let it go quickly when the sea sucked it back; you couldn't fight the ocean.

Then came a big wave, crashing over the reef, drenching Thomas and Molly but leaving them miraculously holding on. And when the wave withdrew the boat was still there, perched precariously on the rocks. Another wave tilted it but pulled back, leaving it where it was. And another, and another. It was settling a little, spiked on a sharp spur of rock which had penetrated the bow. The next few waves hardly moved it.

Thomas ducked under the outrigger, got his hands to the side of the canoe, and pulled himself up. He found himself staring across at Molly. Between them, the well of the boat had already some inches of water in it. And two . . . people? Or bodies?

The eyes and lips of one of them moved.

They were people, living people. Just.

But there was no time to think about them. A big wave tilted the boat dangerously forward. Molly and Thomas clung to the gunwales. Molly was as wet now as her brother, and impeded by heavy soaked clothing. And suddenly they became aware – having heard nothing against the sea-noise that filled their ears – that Dan and Jemmy were swimming out from the shore to join them.

Jemmy had a start, but Dan overhauled him and in a minute stood on a rock beside Molly. Dan, strong and solid. Dan, gesturing across the boat to Thomas, shouting something that couldn't be heard, but of which there was no mistaking the meaning. Together they heaved at the canoe, trying to lift it off the spiking rock and over the reef.

They couldn't do it. The boat was light, but with two people in it and an increasing weight of water it was more than they could lift.

Jemmy clutched at Thomas's ankles. Thomas helped him up from the water to a precarious foothold. They all tried together to raise the boat, but still they could barely move it.

Then came a huge wave, as big as the one that had planted it on the reef. They could see the wave from a hundred yards away, moving in. Dan signalled to the others to wait for their chance. At the moment of its arrival, the four of them strained with all their strength. The boat rose from the rock and pitched forward, carrying them with it. In a whirl of weight and water, Molly was submerged, felt the boat hit her shoulder, thought she was drowning, and then was on the surface, impeded by her wet clothes, but swimming.

And there, not far away from her, were the others: three heads bobbing on the surface of the quiet water to landward of the reef. The boat, its rags of sail catching the wind, had left them behind. By the time they had swum ashore, it was aground on the black sand.

Not waiting to squeeze sea water from their clothes, the four of them looked into the canoe. Molly looked away quickly. The occupants were not a pretty sight. They were almost naked. Their cheeks and eyes were sunken, their limbs wasted, and the outlines of bones clearly visible through the skin. There were bruises, cuts and sores all over their bodies.

Molly forced herself to look again. Now she saw that the people in the boat were both young: a boy and girl, probably no more than in mid teens like herself and Thomas and Dan, and smaller-boned. The girl appeared to be unconscious. As Molly watched, the boy opened his eyes and moved his tongue over cracked and swollen lips. He tried to speak, but only a faint croaking sound emerged. There was no sign of food or drink in the boat, though there were empty gourds which had probably held water. Molly leaned over, picked up one of these and handed it to Thomas.

'Run and fetch some water,' she said. 'You ain't hampered by clothes as much as I am.'

Thomas brought water from one of the tiny springs that ran out of crevices in the cliffs. Molly offered it to the boy's lips. He drank with difficulty, then tried to drag himself up from the floor of the boat. Dan and Thomas helped him prop himself higher, and he drank again. The girl was staring blankly at the sky, apparently unconscious, but when Molly wetted two fingers and put them to the dry lips there was an involuntary sucking movement. Molly went on trying, and got a little water into the girl's mouth. Her eyes moved and focussed, and a minute later there was a painful-seeming, convulsive movement of the throat, suggesting that she had swallowed.

'Who are you?' Dan asked the boy. There was no reply. Dan leaned over and put his face closer. 'Who are you?' he repeated.

The boy shook his head.

'Are you deaf?' Dan demanded loudly.

The boy shook his head again.

'Then answer me!' Dan told him. But there was no reply. Dan was beginning to get cross.

'If you're not deaf, you can answer me!' he said.

Molly plucked at Dan's sleeve.

'He's ill,' she said. 'I think he's frightened. And maybe he can't speak. Let me try.'

'Are you feeling any better?' she asked the boy. 'Don't answer, just nod your head.'

But the boy shook his head again. The girl groaned. The boy turned toward her, and in a hoarse voice whispered something incomprehensible.

'That ain't English!' Molly exclaimed, surprised.

'Well!' said Dan. 'He don't even speak English. What d'you make of that?'

Molly shook her head. She had never before heard anyone speak a language that wasn't English.

'You know what?' said Dan in a significant tone. 'They're incomers. That's what they are. Incomers!'

'What if they are?' said Thomas.

'You know what the Teaching says about incomers.'

'They're evil!' exclaimed nine-year-old Jemmy, excited. 'Sent by the Bad One!'

'That's a lot of nonsense,' said Thomas.

'Nonsense? The Teaching? *Nonsense?*' Dan was shocked.

'Whoever they are and wherever they're from,' said Molly, 'I reckon they're cold, and starving, and we got to do something about it.'

'Do what?' asked Dan.

'Get them out of the boat. And cover them up.'

'They could do with *that*,' Dan said, looking disapprovingly at the nearly-naked bodies.

'Everything we have is wet,' said Thomas. 'It won't be any help to them.'

'Poor things,' said Molly.

'Poor things?' repeated Jemmy, round-eyed. 'Incomers! Poor things?'

Molly was offering them more water. Both drank, but the girl was still very feeble. She turned her head aside and closed her eyes. The boy now said something to Molly. He spoke clearly and distinctly, but his words had no meaning for her. She smiled and shook her head.

The boy pointed to his mouth.

'He wants something to eat,' Thomas said.

'He'll have to want, then, won't he?' said Dan.

'We could give him an egg,' Molly said. 'Where are they, Dan?'

'They're in my bag over there. But who says we can give him an egg? The Reader wouldn't allow it.'

'The Reader doesn't know how many eggs you have,' said Thomas.

'No,' said Dan, 'but . . .'

'Go on, give him an egg,' said Molly.

'I'll give him an egg if you'll give *me* a kiss,' suggested Dan.

'Well, I won't,' said Molly. 'You haven't the right. You ain't asked for me yet, and if you did I mightn't take you. Anyway, we got plenty to do without kissing. Give me that egg.'

'Here's one from *my* bag, Moll,' said Jemmy. He was interested. 'Do incomers eat eggs?'

'I don't know,' said Molly. 'We'll see.'

She broke an egg into Thomas's cupped hands. They showed it to the boy, who looked unsure about it.

'You see?' Dan said. 'Waste of an egg. Good job the Reader don't know.'

'Show him what to do,' Thomas suggested.

Dan didn't need asking twice. He sucked up the raw egg from Thomas's hands, and made appreciative noises by way of instructing the castaway. Molly broke another egg, and this time the boy swallowed it, though pulling a face. He spoke in his own tongue to the girl, who opened her eyes, turned toward him, replied in a barely audible voice, and turned away again.

'She don't want one,' Dan said. 'Just as well, eh, seeing we ain't offered her one.'

Thomas looked as if about to say something, but didn't speak.

'Well, what we going to do with 'em?' Dan went on. 'Can we get them to the village?' He turned again to the boy, and asked in a loud voice, 'Can you walk? WALK?' But the boy only looked bewildered.

Dan made signals to him to get up. This time the boy understood and tried to raise himself, but was obviously too feeble. He sank back.

'They can't even get up,' said Molly, 'never mind walk.'

Dan scratched his head, baffled.

'Maybe somebody from the village saw the boat come in,' said Jemmy. 'Maybe they'll be arriving soon.'

'*That's* not likely,' Molly said. 'Not with the headland and part of the Peak in the way.' And then, after a moment, 'We're not far from Uncle Abel's cave. Why don't we try and take them there?'

'Just what I was going to suggest,' said Dan. 'Let's see if we can move them.'

They got the boy out of the boat first. With his arms round the shoulders of Molly and Thomas, one on each side of him, he managed to walk in a weak, tottering way. But there was clearly no chance that the girl could walk. She was awake now, and watching them with frightened eyes. Dan picked her up and slung her across his shoulders, hardly seeming to notice her slight weight.

'All right,' he said. 'Abel's cave, then. It'll be a surprise for the old feller, won't it, supposing he's at home. And when we've took 'em there, we'll pull that boat above the high water mark. I want to have a look at it. In the meantime, just you keep out of it, young Jemmy.'

Jemmy, who had scrambled into the canoe, scrambled guiltily out again. The little procession straggled for half a mile along the narrow, boulder-strewn beach, past the opening of a gulch that ran down from the Peak, and as far as the cave where old Abel Oakes lived alone.

The cave had two round openings, high above ground level, which, seen in conjunction with a bulge in the rock-face, gave it a skull-like look; it was sometimes known as Skull Cave. Thomas and Molly, with the boy held between them, led the way in through its mouth. Inside was a large front compartment, some five or six yards square, and well lit by daylight through the two sockets. Here Abel lived and kept his few possessions. There was also a black inner area, opening into the depths of the cliff, where nobody but Abel ever went.

'Abel!' bawled Dan. 'Uncle Abel!'

There was no reply.

'He's out,' Dan said. 'Oh well, never mind. Saves argument.'

There was a pile of dirty old bedding in a corner of the cave. Dan dumped the girl on it unceremoniously. Molly and Thomas laid the boy gently beside her. The brief walk seemed to have exhausted him. His head fell sideways on to the folded, smelly sheepskin that Abel used as a pillow. His eyes were open, but he didn't move or speak.

'Cover 'em up,' said Dan. 'They ain't decent.' Then, 'You come out of that inner cave, young Jemmy! Always nosing around, aren't you? Stay here, where I can keep an eye on you.'

'I don't want to hurt their sores,' said Thomas, looking down at the two incomers.

'But they're perished with cold,' Molly said.

With great care Thomas drew more of Abel's bedding over the two inert bodies.

'Now we better go and tell them at the village,' he said.

'Ain't no hurry,' said Dan. 'I want to have a proper look at that boat.'

'Our mum ought to see them, maybe,' suggested Molly. 'She knows about nursing.'

'You go along, then,' Dan said. 'You and Thomas. It won't make no difference in the end, you know. Recover or die, it won't matter. The Reader won't have them.'

Then there was movement in the low mouth of the cave. An old man ducked into it and stood, affronted, inside. They hadn't heard him approaching barefoot over the sand.

'What you lot doing in here?' demanded Uncle Abel.

Abel Oakes was small and spare, with thick white hair and furrowed, deeply suntanned face. He was eighty at least, and had long qualified for the title of 'Uncle,' conferred by islanders on all elderly men; but his sight and hearing were excellent and he had all his teeth.

Abel had married his cousin Jess when he was twenty and she was eighteen. Two years later she'd died in childbirth; the child had died, too. Since then, for longer than all but a few of the oldest islanders could remember, he'd lived here as a recluse, four miles from the village. He had his vegetable plot at this end of the flatland, and owned a few sheep and hens. Like everyone else, he fished, ate eggs and young seabirds, and collected shellfish. Uncle Abel was harmless, but he rarely spoke to anyone, and unlike almost every other islander he didn't go to the meeting-place on Prayer Day.

Today he was angry.

'Nobody ain't allowed in here without I say so!' he declared. 'And I ain't said so to you!' Then his eye fell on the two incomers. The boy had seen him, and was struggling up toward a sitting position.

'Who are they?' Abel demanded.

'How would I know?' said Dan sullenly. 'We just pulled them off the reef, that's all. I'm surprised you didn't see us.'

'I been working my plot,' said Abel. 'Seems I can't turn my back without something happening.' He approached the boy and girl and drew back the foul bedding that Thomas had placed over them. Then he asked the boy, in gentler tones,

'Where you from?'

The boy shook his head.

'He don't take it in,' said Dan. 'He don't even speak English. They got here in that canoe that's out there on the beach, what's left of it. Must've come a long way, I reckon.'

Abel was looking at the pair with interest.

'A long way?' he repeated. 'Aye, there's no doubt about that. They've come a thousand miles, at least. They must've done, 'cause there ain't no land nearer. It's a miracle they made it. If they'd missed us, they'd 'a' been blown another thousand. Not that they'd have survived that.'

'A thousand miles!' Molly exclaimed softly. It was an impressive phrase, though it didn't really mean much to her. Halcyon was just seven miles long and five miles wide, and most of it was taken up by the Peak.

She knew there were places where other people lived, of course. Six years ago, when she was only a little girl, a ship had dropped anchor a mile off the shore where the village was. The sea being quieter than usual, it had managed to send a boat ashore. The sailors had traded clothing, tea and tobacco for potatoes, eggs and fresh mutton. They'd brought liquor, too, but the Halcyon elders had sent that back; strong drink was not allowed on the island. They'd promised to bring a bit of timber and some nails and screws, which Halcyon needed most of all, but for the next week the weather had been too rough, and then the ship had sailed away without another landing. That ship was all that Molly Reeves had seen of the outside world.

'I seen a young man like this before,' Abel went on. 'Same colouring, same shape of face, same everything, and spoke a lingo we couldn't understand. He was saved from a wreck, I think. I was only a lad at the time.'

'What happened to him?' Thomas asked.

'Rejected, like the Book says. The Reader − old Josh Wilde it was then − had him put on Kingfisher Island, and we never saw him again. He hadn't a boat, of course, and nothing to make one with. I don't know how long he lasted.

My Jess was quite upset. Soft-hearted, she was. I can't say I liked it much myself.'

'That's what'll happen to these two, isn't it?' said Thomas.

'I reckon so. That's if they don't die first.'

'But you couldn't just let them *die*!' Molly exclaimed.

'I'm not going to, me dear,' said Abel. 'It's not for me to say what happens in the end. But just for now, I'll keep 'em alive if I can. That's what my Jess would have done. So, young Thomas, fetch me that jug o' water over there, and my mug.'

The girl stirred, licking her lips. The boy put out a hand and touched hers. Thomas gave each of them a little water.

'Does the Reader have to know about them?' Molly asked.

'Where's your wits, Moll?' demanded Dan. 'Of course the Reader and elders have to know. Do you think you could *hide* them, in a place the size of Halcyon? And the boat as well?'

'Now, now!' said the old man. 'Off you go, all of you. Get out of my place. I still ain't given you leave to be here, remember.' He looked down at the young pair.

'I reckon they'll survive,' he said, 'but they need nourishing, and a bit of care. I don't mind Hester Reeves coming; she's a good woman and knows how to look after folk. But you can tell them at the village, I don't want none of the rest of them here, least of all the Reader. These two won't get away.'

His face softened.

'They're only young,' he said. 'They need caring for. That's what my Jess would have done – cared for them.'

Molly was sure there was a tear in his eye. Not for the incomers but for his Jess, dead sixty years, and the children they might have had.

'Come on, then,' said Dan. 'Molly, you and Thomas can go home. Jemmy and me will finish getting eggs – we've nearly got 'em all already – and have a look at that boat.'

Jemmy was still excited as they left the cave.

'The Bad One sent them, didn't he?' he said. 'They'll have to be put away, won't they?'

'Don't be stupid, Jemmy Kane!' said Thomas.

'Stupid yourself!' retorted Jemmy, who wasn't afraid of him.

'Be quiet, both of you!' Molly told them. But when she and Thomas were on the way home she said thoughtfully,

'They're just a boy and girl like us, aren't they? It couldn't *really* be the Bad One that sent them, could it, Thomas?'

''Course it couldn't!' said Thomas. 'But I bet we haven't heard the last of that.'

Chapter 2

*I*T was dusk when Molly and Thomas got home. Lamplight flickered fraily from the scattered windows of the village. Somewhere a couple of dogs barked at each other. The wind blew, as always, carrying across the upland the sound of the surf, the cries of seabirds, and a touch and taste of spray.

Thomas pushed open the door of the Reeveses' cottage, and he and Molly went in. Their father, Dick Reeves, a thin, wiry man, sat at one side of the big fireplace. Opposite him were his elder daughter Beth, a year older than Molly but smaller and slighter, and Adam Goodall, whom Beth was to marry. Adam was in his early twenties: a well-built young islander, a good man in a boat, quiet and, some said, deep. A pot sat on an iron grid over the fire.

'About time you were here!' Dick Reeves grumbled to Thomas. 'Your mother was beginning to wonder if you was all right. What with you a poor climber and your sister running wild just like a lad . . .'

'Now, now, Dick,' chided Hester Reeves, a cheerful, capable woman, half a head taller than her husband. 'I wasn't worrying at all. They just timed it right. Supper's ready this minute.' And then, in a startled tone, to Molly,

'Come here, girl! Your clothes is all wet. Why, you're soaked through! What you been up to? And Thomas, you're as bad!'

'We rescued two people!' Thomas announced. 'Us and Dan and Jemmy. Molly and me was there first!'

'Rescued two people!' their father exclaimed. 'Who?'

'Strangers.'

'Strangers? What do you mean, strangers? There's no strangers on Halcyon!'

'They're not from Halcyon!'

'Not . . . somebody from the Outside World?' asked Beth, round-eyed.

'Yes!' Thomas was gratified by the reception of his news. His father got up from the fireside and came over to them, full of curiosity.

'What are they?' he demanded. 'Sailors? Castaways? How did they get here? How old are they? Where are they now?'

Thomas told him.

'They're poorly,' Molly added. 'The girl, specially.'

'They were dying of thirst,' Thomas said. 'And starving too, I dare say.'

'And, mum, Uncle Abel says you better go and see them, seeing you know about nursing,' said Molly.

'Oh, *that's* what Abel says, is it?' said Dick Reeves sourly. 'Since when does Abel Oakes tell us what to do? I reckon he's out of his wits, from living alone in that cave. They say he spends hours on end talking to his wife, as if she was still alive. And isn't it just like him, when he'll never let any of *us* in, that he'll take in newcomers from Deliverer-knows-where? Wasting time and trouble.'

'Uncle Abel has more sense than people think,' said Adam quietly.

'Oh, I do hope those two are all right!' said Molly.

'You might as well save your hopes for something useful!' her father told her.

'But they need help!' Molly cried. 'If you could see their poor thin bruised bodies . . .'

'Why, girl, I believe you're blubbering!' Hester Reeves exclaimed.

'I'm not!' said Molly, but it wasn't true. She swallowed and tried to stifle a sob, but couldn't.

'You great soft thing!' her mother said, not without sympathy. 'You used to be like that when animals got hurt, when you was a little girl. Well, I'll do what I can, but I can't get to Abel's cave tonight: four miles each way in the dark, and all those gulches to cross. I'll go tomorrow.'

'Not unless the Reader says so, you won't!' said Dick Reeves sharply.

'I don't see why not,' Hester said.

'Well, I'm telling you. I'm head of the household, aren't I? You know what the Teaching says. A man will keep his wife and children under control, and they're to do his bidding. I'm standing by that. You won't have nothing to do with incomers except the Reader says you can. I don't want no trouble, and I'll thank my family to toe the line.'

'I think it's time all that was changed,' said Beth.

'You keep a respectful tongue in your head, my girl,' her father told her. 'While you're in my house, you'll behave yourself and speak civil. After you're wed, it'll be up to Adam to keep you in order.'

'Adam thinks like I do,' said Beth.

Adam nodded. Dick Reeves glared.

'There, let's stop all this arguing,' said Hester Reeves peaceably. 'We'll see what the Reader says tomorrow. Now, come on, Molly, eat your supper. You'll feel better after that.'

'But those poor people . . .' Molly began.

'You heard!' snapped her father.

'What is it for supper? Stew again?' Thomas asked.

'Yes, it's stew again. And getting a bit thin, I'm afraid. I'm thankful there's still plenty of potatoes,' said Hester.

'Not plenty,' said her husband. 'Some.'

'Eggs are beginning now,' said Thomas.

'Yes. And where's the ones you was collecting today?'

'Dan and Jemmy have them. Don't worry, we'll get our share.'

'I guess so. How'd you get on? Did you climb?'

'Thomas climbed right down Sammy's Cliff when we saw the boat coming in,' Molly said quickly. 'He led the way down.' She knew her father felt contempt for Thomas because he couldn't stand heights. But then, mentioning the boat, she was reminded again of the strangers, the desperate state they were in and their probable fate; and she found herself weeping again.

'You're tired, Molly lass,' her mother said. 'Sup up that stew, and then I reckon you better go to bed.'

'Look at her clothes,' said Beth. 'She needs to change out of those.'

'I ain't got no others,' Molly said.

'We got enough between us,' said Beth. 'You can wear my spare petticoat for a start.'

That was a generous offer.

'Thank you, Beth,' said Molly. 'I hope it's big enough.'

'As for you, Adam,' said Hester, 'it's time you was going. You can't stay here with ladies changing clothes. That's not a sight for your eyes. You ain't married *yet*.'

Beth and Molly both blushed.

'You keep tossing and turning,' Beth said later. 'That ain't comfortable to be in bed with. I wish you'd go to sleep.'

'Oh, Beth, you should have *seen* them!' said Molly, still thinking of the incomers. 'It was dreadful. And I'm that worried.'

'No good worrying,' said Beth. 'Try not to think about it.'

'But I can't help thinking about it.'

Molly lay awake, continued to toss and turn, and wept a little. Beth slept a while, then woke and put her arms round Molly.

'There, there,' she said. 'You're getting too big to be a little sister. A great strong girl like you!'

Molly was obscurely comforted, and in the end slept heavily. When she woke again, it was long past first light, and Beth was gone. Molly got out of bed and wandered, rubbing her eyes, into the main living-space. Sunlight was coming in through the deep narrow windows. Her mother gave her milk and some cold potato.

'Lovely day,' she said. 'The men are all gone to the fishing. They was off before dawn.'

'I didn't hear the call.'

'You was sleeping heavy, I reckon. Thomas heard it and

got up, though he don't have to go. He'd be willing, you know; he don't mind the sea like he does the cliffs. I tell him he'll have to go soon enough.'

'Where *is* Thomas?'

'I'm here,' Thomas said, appearing from the back of the house. 'Been milking Daisy.'

'I keep thinking about them two from the canoe,' Molly told him. 'I been thinking about them all night.'

'Except when you was asleep,' said Thomas.

'I was sort of thinking about them even when I was asleep. What's going to happen next?'

'Well, Dan and his dad are both off in the boats,' said Hester Reeves. 'I dare say nobody's told the Reader yet. But he'll soon hear about it. You better stay and help me, Molly. Thomas, you see to the animals. I don't want either of you going up to the vegetable plots, in case you're needed.'

Hester was right. News of the arrivals got around rapidly. Rebecca Wilde, Dan's mother, was soon out telling her neighbours. The story passed around the village from house to house, and little knots of women stood in the open discussing it. Soon after Molly had eaten, Abby Jonas came running down from the Reader's house.

'Molly and Thomas!' she cried. 'My grandpa . . .' Then she stopped and corrected herself. 'I mean, the Reader wants to see you!'

Abby was the daughter of Isaac Jonas, the Reader's son. Isaac had been drowned with half a dozen others when the island's best boat, *Petrel*, was lost four years earlier. Abby was the Reader's only grandchild, and the consolation of his old age. She was slim, bright-eyed and dark-haired, and envied by Molly for her slenderness. She was thought to like Thomas, and there was some speculation in the village as to whether Dick Reeves would venture to ask for her for his son. Island opinion was that Abby was too spoiled and insufficiently sturdy to be an ideal wife, but that, as the Reader's granddaughter, she would nonetheless be a good match for a Reeves.

Now she led the way importantly to the Reader's house,

which was the best in the village and flagship of the little fleet of long low homes that lay on the upland like ships at anchor in a harbour. Its windows faced into the hillside. If they'd been in the opposite wall there would have been fine views of the sea; but Halcyon islanders saw enough of the sea without wanting to look at it when they were safe at home.

The Reader's house was slightly bigger than the rest. It had a boarded floor, instead of the trodden earth of the others, and in the living-room were three wooden chairs, a broken-down armchair, and a stout joiner-made table, acquired in some long-forgotten deal with a passing ship. A kettle simmered on the iron grid over the fire.

The Reader, William Jonas, was an islander of middle height and rather bulky, having put on weight since he stopped going out sea-fishing. At seventy-nine he was older than he liked to hear mentioned. His face had not expanded to match his body, and now looked small; his eyes were narrow, watery and close together, his hair thinning. He wore an enormous woollen jersey, old stained trousers and a venerable pair of island-made sheepskin slippers; and he sat, stick in hand, in the ancient armchair. Beside and slightly to the rear of him sat his sharp-faced sister Sarah.

'Now, Thomas,' the Reader said, by way of greeting. 'Now, Molly.'

Thomas made an awkward bow, and Molly a curtsey.

'I'm told you have news for us,' the Reader said. There was curiosity in his eyes. Sarah Jonas, looking equally curious, edged forward. Abby peered from a dark corner of the room. News on Halcyon was a rare commodity.

'Yes,' said Thomas nervously, and hesitated.

'Well, come on, then. Out with it!'

Thomas collected himself and told the story, with two or three additions from Molly. Everyone listened intently.

'So Abel's looking after them!' said William Jonas, when Thomas had finished. 'And he wants your mother to go down there!'

'He would!' said Sarah in a disapproving tone. 'That's Abel Oakes all over!'

27

'Don't speak too soon, me dear,' William told her. 'If there's trouble to be took, it may as well be took by Abel as anybody else. And I don't mind Hester Reeves going down there. It wouldn't do no harm for them to recover enough for us to find out where they come from, and why.'

'But you heard what Thomas and Molly said. They don't speak no proper language. We won't find anything out from them.'

'They do need caring for,' Molly said. For the hundredth time the picture of the two bruised, emaciated bodies came before her eyes. 'I just hope they haven't . . . you know . . .'

'Died,' said Thomas.

'That might be the best thing that could happen,' William said.

'But . . . they're only young, like us.'

'They're from Outside,' William said sternly. Sarah nodded vigorously in emphasis. 'You know what the Teaching is.'

'I don't,' Thomas said. 'At least, not properly. I've heard folk talk about it, but I don't know if they got it right.'

'You don't know the Teaching?' William Jonas straightened himself up in his chair. He always liked to tell people about the Teaching. 'Well, you can't expect to know *all* the Teaching, not at your age, but you ought to know the parts that we're concerned with now. And to begin with, young man, the Teaching comes from the Book, and the person in charge of the Book is the Reader, and the Reader is me.'

'But you can't read it, can you?' Thomas asked.

Sarah Jonas leaned forward and looked for a moment as if she would slap Thomas's face.

'Impudence!' she exclaimed.

'But . . . you can't, can you, Mr Jonas?' Thomas said to the Reader in a small voice, keeping his distance from Sarah. 'Nobody on Halcyon can read.'

'That's as may be, young man,' said William. 'I don't require to read the Book in order to tell you the Teaching. I know the Teaching all ways, upside down and backwards and forwards. I know it by heart. I had it from the Reader before me, and he had it from the Reader before him, and *he* had it from the Reader before *him* . . .'

William paused, to allow his words to have their cumulative effect.

'And you only have to go back through another two or three Readers,' he finished triumphantly, 'and you come to the Deliverer himself! Yes, young Thomas, the Teaching has Authority. And the authority it has is that of the Deliverer: of that same Joseph Kane that brought our forebears safe and sound to Halcyon, and delivered them from sin!'

Sarah Jonas nodded sharply, as if her chin were striking little hammer-blows of emphasis.

'Now it's true,' William added, 'that we don't have the art of reading. Takes a lot of working at, that does, and we've enough to do keeping ourselves alive. And from what's been handed down to me, it seems that maybe the Deliverer himself wasn't all that anxious that folk should read. After all, it ain't important, is it? Reading don't catch no fish, nor stop no sin. So long as we know what the Teaching says, we know all we need to know.'

'That's right!' said Sarah.

'And I got every word of it *here*!' said William. He pointed to his chest; then, after consideration, to his head. 'Better than reading, because I don't have to go to the Meeting-House and turn over pages and all that. I can bring it straight to mind, whichever bit I want.'

'He can that!' said Sarah.

'Now let me tell you what the Teaching says about what we're concerned with. As a start, it's laid down in the Book that the first duty of all of us is to avoid evil.'

'Which is what William Jonas has done all his life,' said his sister.

'I think I can truthfully say that,' the Reader agreed modestly. 'And I may say, it ain't no easy matter, avoiding evil. The Bad One whispers in the ears of all of us sometimes. Even, believe it or not, in mine!'

'But of course William don't listen!' Sarah added.

'He may even have spoke in *your* ears. It ain't my present duty to inquire. I reckon he must talk pretty loud in the ears of some, like Bob Attwood with his bad temper and Harry Kane with his laziness — and Harry bearing the honoured name of the Deliverer, too . . .' The Reader broke off, confused. 'Where had I got to?'

'Avoiding evil,' said Thomas.

'Oh, yes. Well, I wouldn't say we're perfect on Halcyon. Not even I am perfect; not quite. But, by and large, I think we keep the Bad One at bay. Of course, if we do sin we get punished for it, like Alec Campbell, that went digging his plot on Prayer Day, contrary to the Teaching, and cut his foot open with the spade.'

'And serve him right!' said Sarah.

'You were going to tell us about incomers,' Thomas said.

'That's right. Now, the Bad One will never rest,' William went on, adopting the tone of one reading a text, 'and forasmuch as the island has been delivered from evil, so much more will the Bad One seek to restore its rule. And let it not be doubted that the Bad One will bring to these shores, when he thinks the time ripe, those whose sins have caused them to be shipwrecked, or to be cast off by them that were their companions, or to roam the world taking wickedness wherever they go. For assuredly shipwreck is a punishment for sin.'

'Wickedness wherever they go!' echoed Sarah with relish. 'Punishment for sin!'

'Therefore, when such persons shall come to the island, let them not be allowed to remain. And if they shall come in boats, let them be taken back to sea in their own boat, and let it be cast adrift without oar or sail, and with food and water for seven days only, and let the Bad One take care of his own.

'But if they shall have no boat, then let not the Islanders provide any boat, for that would be to do the Bad One's work. Let such persons rather be carried to the isle known as Kingfisher, and there left with seven days' food and water, and let no Islander have any further dealing with them or otherwise set foot on that isle, for it is a place of evil.'

'There you are, you see,' said Sarah. 'A place of evil. That's why we sometimes call it Sin Island.' She rolled the phrase round her lips, secure in the consciousness of her own virtue.

'Now didn't you know of this?' the Reader inquired.

'We had heard it,' Thomas admitted.

'So you know what must be done. Seems to me we got no choice. It's the Teaching.'

'We shall cast out evil!' Sarah declared with satisfaction.

'And we better do it quickly,' the Reader said. 'Because while ever they're here, we don't know what the Bad One might be doing through them.' He paused for a moment, then added thoughtfully, 'All the same, I don't think this is for me to decide alone. The people got to make this decision. I shall call an Island Meeting.'

Molly, who had been increasingly depressed as the Reader's explanation went on, now felt a slight gleam of hope.

'Those two didn't look evil,' she said. 'They looked nice.'

'And they couldn't say anything bad,' said Thomas, 'because they don't speak our language. They couldn't do us any harm.'

'Are you arguing with your elders and betters?' the Reader demanded.

'No, but . . .'

'Oh, if you could have seen them!' said Molly. 'Their eyes and lips and their poor thin arms and legs!'

'That's the Bad One all over!' cried Sarah triumphantly. 'He'll try to make you sorry for his creatures. Oh, he knows what he's doing all right! And if they speak his language and not that of decent folk, there's a reason for it, you can be sure!'

'A pity the men are all out fishing today,' said the Reader meditatively. 'Of course, we can't afford to waste good weather. Deliverer knows, we need the food; we only just got through this last winter. Seems to me we better wait till Prayer Day, when there's no fishing, then send a boat round the shore to bring them here; they won't be fit to go overland.

And we'll have the Island Meeting the same day. Dealing with incomers on Prayer Day can't be sinful, can it, Sarah? It's doing the Deliverer's work.'

'I'm sure you know best what is and isn't sinful, William,' said Sarah. 'If you say it isn't, it isn't.'

'I reckon you're right,' said William complacently. 'And I say it's not sinful. We'll bring their boat round at the same time. Tell me about that boat, Thomas.'

'It's a funny affair,' Thomas said. 'With a sort of float stuck out to one side.'

'An outrigger. Those folk must have come far. From way over east, I reckon. And that's the way the wind would bring them, this time of year. Yes, it all makes sense.'

'The boat's stove in,' said Thomas. 'It'd take quite a lot of mending. And I don't know what it's made of. Nothing we've got, I think.'

'It's not fit to set them adrift in, then?' asked the Reader.

Suddenly Molly couldn't restrain herself. She flared up.

'You can't set them adrift!' she cried. 'You can't, Mr Jonas! It's not . . . it's not human!'

'And it's not right,' Thomas added, his voice nervous but determined. 'They haven't done any harm.'

The Reader rose bulkily to his feet.

'*You* tell *me* what's right?' he said. 'You think you know better than the Book?'

'Ought to be flogged, both of them!' declared Sarah.

'We don't flog young women on this island,' said William, 'even if they deserve it. As for you, Thomas . . . well, you're not the strongest lad on Halcyon. I won't have you beaten; I'll just tell your dad about the way you've behaved and leave it to him. Every man shall keep his family under control, that's the Teaching.'

'Let no one forget it!' observed Sarah.

'And, Molly Reeves,' the Reader went on, 'it seems to me that you need to learn what a woman's place is. You been chasing around like a lad too long. Time you stayed at home and found out how to card and spin and sew and knit and wash and cook and clean and all the other jobs that's only fit for women, ready for when you get married. I shall tell your parents that. You wouldn't find my Abby running around barefoot all over the island like you do . . . Where is she? Where's my lovey?'

'I'm here, Grandpa,' said Abby from the shadows.

'I hope you listened to that, Abby, and took it all in,' the Reader said. 'I hope you'll always be better behaved and more respectful than Molly and Thomas.'

'I hope so too, Grandpa,' said Abby. She came forward and give him a winning smile. The Reader beamed fondly on her. Molly dug her fingernails into her palms to prevent herself from hitting Abby, hard.

Chapter 3

HESTER Reeves set off for Abel's cave as soon as she heard that the Reader had no objection. She took salves and dressings with her, and some fresh goat's milk. Molly and Thomas were left behind to await their father's return from fishing. Thomas, astonished by his own audacity, grew more apprehensive as the day wore on; Molly was boiling up slowly into a state of high indignation with William and Sarah Jonas.

Dick Reeves came in a little later than expected, accompanied by Adam Goodall, who was a member of the same crew. It was obvious at once that Dick had already been told of the interview with the Reader, and wasn't pleased about it.

'I hear you was impertinent and speaking out of turn,' he said. 'Answering the Reader back! Thomas, you're the eldest. What do you have to say for yourself?'

Thomas licked his lips nervously and didn't say anything.

'William left it to me,' his father said. 'But Sarah Jonas says I ought to give you the strap. She says that young folk are getting out of hand. When she was your age, she says . . .'

'We always did as we was told,' said Molly in a mimicking voice.

'That'll do, Molly. You been impudent enough already for one day. Maybe Sarah's right. Maybe I've not been firm enough with my children.'

Adam Goodall spoke up.

'Beg your pardon, Dick,' he said. 'But I know why Molly and Thomas were upset. I don't like setting folk adrift that haven't done us any harm, any more than they do.'

'It's in the Teaching,' Dick Reeves said.

'I know. Or so we're told. But maybe the Teaching isn't everything. Maybe the Teaching doesn't have it right.'

'The Teaching's what we live by,' Dick said. 'And always have done. After all, most of it's common sense, ain't it? The Teaching tells us to work together and help our neighbour and all that; and how could we live on Halcyon if we didn't? And it tells us to look after them that gets hurt or old or ill, and of course it's right, it's looking after ourselves really, because we might be the next ones that needs looking after. And it tells us to share when we kills a sheep or when we're the only ones with taters left, and to give back what we borrows, and to see that our wives does what they're told. Nothing wrong with any of that, is there?'

'No, but . . .'

'It tells us to keep our children in order, too,' said Dick, looking meaningfully at Thomas.

'That's all very well, Dick,' said Adam. 'But when it goes on about the Bad One, and folk that cast the Evil Eye and so on, I can't agree with it.'

'But you *got* to agree with the Teaching,' said Dick uneasily. 'It's been proved over and over again. Remember when a boat went out on Prayer Day and capsized? And Alec Campbell's foot? And remember old Nelly Oakes? *She* used to cast the Evil Eye, there ain't no doubt about it. Whoever she cast it on, their sheep got scab and their taters got blight, and when she was put away on Kingfisher it all stopped. And as for incomers . . .'

'When did incomers ever do us any harm?' asked Adam.

'They never been allowed to!' said Dick triumphantly.

The door opened and Hester Reeves came in.

'Still going on about it?' she asked. 'Well, if you want to know, I think like Molly and Thomas. It ain't right to do harm to folk that haven't done any to us. And as for setting them adrift, I can't abide the thought.'

'If people kept coming and was allowed to stay, there'd be more mouths to feed,' said Dick, 'and we have trouble enough feeding the mouths we have already.'

'Well, now, perhaps we're coming to the point,' said Adam. 'More mouths to feed, yes. Maybe *that's* what lies behind the Teaching.'

But Dick Reeves was tired of the discussion. He yawned hugely.

'It's been a hard day at the fishing,' he said. 'And another tomorrow if the weather holds. Let's stop arguing and have our supper. A man's entitled to take it easy at his own fireside.'

Adam looked as if he had more to say. Hester Reeves put a hand on his shoulder.

'Stay and eat with us, Adam,' she said. 'And calm yourself down. And you too, Molly. I can see you all bubbling up inside. It's no good getting upset.'

'Anyway, how *are* they?' asked Molly.

'I made them comfortable. They'll be all right. They're not going to die, I promise you. But why didn't you tell me about that awful bedding of Abel's? I can't leave them in that; it's filthy. I have some clean stuff I can lend, but I don't know how I'm going to get it down there.'

'We'll take it after supper,' Molly offered at once.

Hester looked inquiringly at her husband, expecting some objection. But Dick Reeves shrugged his shoulders.

'If the Reader ain't forbidden it,' he said, 'I'm not going to. At least there'll be a bit of peace and quiet here.'

'It's a tricky walk in the dark,' said Hester.

'Me and Adam will go too,' said Beth. 'With four of us all together, there won't be no accidents.'

'I'll bring them back all right,' said Adam. He smiled engagingly at Hester.

'Oh, *you*!' said Hester. 'You'd charm a bird off a ledge, you would, Adam Goodall. Go on, eat your suppers and be off with you. But don't be too long away.'

It wasn't really dark. The night was clear, with a nearly-full moon. As always and everywhere on Halcyon, the sound and smell of the sea filled the air. The Peak brooded above.

Thomas and Molly hurried ahead, while Beth and Adam

followed arm-in-arm. Their path soon left the village and crossed the grassy upland. At the edge of this, away from all the rest, was an abandoned house. Its roof had fallen in and its timbers had long since been removed, but the carcase of stone remained. Halcyon was short of timber but it wasn't short of stone. That house was known as Jonathan Wilde's, though there hadn't been a Jonathan in the Wilde family for generations. There was a vague belief on the island that something dreadful had happened there long ago, probably in the unknown era before the Deliverer freed Halcyon from sin. Some said the house was haunted. Molly shuddered as she walked past.

The grassland ended, and there was a brief walk along the cliff: a dangerous place, for bits of it often crumbled away, and sudden sharp gusts of wind had been known to sweep people over the edge. Then the path turned inland, and they were on volcanic slopes, crossed by a series of deep gulches. The pattern was always the same: a swift run or slide down to the bottom of the gulch, a stream to be leaped, and then a scramble up the other side, clinging to whatever jutting stone or tuft of coarse grass you could find.

At the fourth of these, known as Billygoat Gulch, they turned down the course of the stream and soon arrived at the shore, having cut off the long distance round the headland. Now it was only a short walk across the sand to Abel's home. Flickering light from his lamp shone weirdly through the eye-sockets of the skull-shaped cave.

Abel responded to Thomas's hail with a suspicious 'Who is it?' But when he saw who his visitors were, he made a welcoming gesture.

'You can come in if you like,' he said. 'And see my children.'

'*Your* children, Abel?'

'Well, not really of course, but they might have been, mightn't they, if only my Jess had lived?'

It occurred to Molly that Abel's children, if he'd had any, would have been middle-aged by now, but she didn't say anything.

The boy and girl had been cleaned up and their sores dressed. The girl was on the ground, covered with Abel's filthy bedding. She did what she could to cooperate as Beth and Molly changed it for the cleaner material sent by Hester Reeves. She was wide awake now, and following every move in the cave with interest. The boy, who had been sitting, struggled to a standing position and came forward. His face broke into a smile.

'We gets on well together, him and me,' said Abel, 'considering that we ain't got a word in common.'

'Nice-looking young fellow, isn't he?' whispered Beth. 'Or will be when he's recovered a bit more. But they're not quite like us, are they?' The incomers' light brown skin colour would not have been unusual among islanders, but their faces were broader, their cheek-bones higher, their noses less prominent, their eyes wide apart with deep brown irises.

The boy stretched out both hands to each of the new arrivals in turn. Then Abel pushed him gently back into a sitting position.

'Weak as a new lamb, he is,' he said. And then,

'I been expecting visitors all day, but only Hester came. I gather old William knows about this, but he ain't being helpful. Is that right, Adam?'

'It is, I'm afraid,' said Adam. 'He says just what you'd expect. According to him, they'll have to go.'

'I won't have it!' the old man declared.

'How're you going to stop it?'

'I don't know, but . . .'

The boy, sensing disturbance in the tones of voice, now looked alarmed. Abel turned toward him, his face softening.

'It's all right,' he said.

The boy smiled again.

'Issawright,' he echoed.

'You hear that? He knows what it means!' said Abel proudly. 'He's learning already! I know his name, too,' He pointed to the boy and said, 'Oh-tee-po!'

'Issawright!' the boy said. 'Otipo!' He pointed in turn at

Abel. 'Ai-bell!' Abel beamed. The boy now pointed to the girl and said 'Mua.' Everyone repeated, 'Moo-ah.' The girl smiled, briefly and faintly.

Thomas sat down between them. This was a game that intrigued him. He pointed to each member of the party in turn, announcing their names in clear distinct tones, which the boy echoed.

'Adam.'

'Ad-dam.'

'Beth.'

'Bess.'

'No. Beth.'

'Bess.'

'No. Beth. Th. Th. Th.'

'Bess.'

'He can't get his tongue round that one, can he?' said Abel indulgently.

'Molly,' said Thomas, moving on.

'Moll-lee.'

'And me, Thomas.'

'Mee-toh-mass.'

'No, just Thomas. Thomas.'

'Toh-mass,' chimed in the girl, her voice so quiet it could hardly be heard. A smile hovered on her lips.

'Issawright!' the boy declared, delighted.

Beth warmed some milk over the fire, and mixed it with egg to give to the newcomers. Thomas went on with the lesson.

'Eggs.'

'Aiggs.'

'Milk.'

'Mill-luk.'

Thomas continued round the cave, pointing in turn to all its sparse contents and naming them. Otipo and Mua repeated the names. The girl's face became almost animated, though her voice was still faint and was soon exhausted. Thomas was impressed by his pupils' progress.

'They must be clever,' he remarked, 'I bet *we* couldn't pick up *their* lingo like that.' The lesson continued for quite a while.

'I wonder if they're brother and sister,' Molly said.

'I can't think of a way to ask them that,' said Thomas after some thought. 'Why are you interested?'

'Because Otipo's so good-looking,' Beth said, teasing. 'There, Molly's blushing.'

'So she is,' said Thomas, mildly surprised.

'I'm not,' said Molly, untruthfully.

'Come on,' Adam said at length. 'Your mum'll be getting worried if we don't start back soon. And, Abel, don't argue when Jacob Wilde and his crew come to collect your youngsters on Prayer Day. Save the arguments for the meeting, eh? I'll go round the village and persuade all the folk I can that we should let them stay. You never know, if enough people think like we do the Reader might find the Teaching means something different from what he's saying at present. William Jonas isn't anyone's fool. And after all, what difference do a couple of young people make?'

'They make a difference to me, all right,' said Abel. 'They make *all* the difference to me. Sinful? Sinful my elbow! Just look at their bright young faces. I trust them more than I do that Jemmy Kane, *or* his dad, I can tell you. All right, Adam, we'll wait for Prayer Day. We're not beat yet. I always was a better man than William Jonas, and I still am, you'll see. It'll be all right.'

'Issawright!' said Otipo happily, recognising the word.

'Little does he know!' said Adam ruefully; and then, 'Good-bye, Otipo. Good-bye, Mua.'

Thomas, Beth and Molly got up to go. Each in turn said 'Good-bye.' The incomers understood. 'Good-bye,' they echoed. 'Good-bye.'

'Amazing, aren't they?' said Thomas. 'I *told* you they're clever.'

'And good-looking,' said Beth. 'Look, Molly's blushing again!'

'Come on, come on!' Adam said, getting his group together. There was disappointment in the incomers' faces as the islanders went out into the night. The last thing the village party saw and heard as they left was Abel trying to make the girl drink up the egg and milk mixture.

'Drink!' he was saying. 'Drink! Like this!' He lifted the tarnished metal cup to his lips, sucked and swallowed with a show of huge enjoyment, then offered it again to the girl, who drank.

'That's right, love,' Abel told her tenderly.

'Issawright!' declared Otipo. 'Issawright!'

Chapter 4

PRAYER-DAY morning brought a clear blue sky and a fresh, mild breeze. The sound of the Calling Bell rang through the village. It was the original ship's bell from the sailing ship *Delivery*, in which the islanders' ancestors had come to Halcyon more than a century earlier, and it was rung with vigour and satisfaction by Luke Jonas, a nephew of the Reader. Luke, an unmarried man of forty, wore a perpetual grin, was clumsily helpful and energetic, and was generally agreed to be likeable but far from bright.

Molly, Beth and Thomas walked to Meeting between their parents. All five of the Reeves family wore the patched but spotlessly clean clothes they kept for best. Molly felt, as always on Prayer Day, uncomfortable and constricted. Over her newly-washed but threadbare woollen underclothes she wore a calico dress, designed for a London lady of different build, and acquired by barter from a sailor some years ago by Molly's grandfather, in exchange for a bag of carrots.

Thomas had on a blue jacket and white, much-mended sailor's trousers, with white woollen stockings pulled up over them to the knees. Molly wore hide moccasins on her usually bare feet; Thomas had the unlucky splendour of an ill-fitting pair of black boots. On any other day, such clothing would have been ridiculed by all young islanders, but on Prayer-Day morning stiff awkward clothes were the universal attire. After midday dinner they would be put away thankfully for another week.

There was an air of excitement in the Meeting-House as the lengthy service got under way. Six men were missing from the gathering, which otherwise included everyone on the island except three or four of the very old and infirm. Among the six were Dan Wilde and his father, Jacob, the Senior Elder. Everyone knew that these six had taken the best boat round the headland to pick up the incomers. There had been hopes that they might be back in time for the service, but there was no sign of them, and William Jonas was not a man to delay the beginning.

'O Deliverer, we come as once you did to this place, to thank you for bringing us out of evil and misery to our fair island of Halcyon . . .' went the familiar words of the opening prayer. There were hymns, handed down from the Deliverer's time and sung energetically but tunelessly from memory, for no islanders had hymn-books or could have read them if they had. There were other prayers, some of which the Reader appeared to be reading from the great leather-bound Book on the lectern in front of him, though everyone knew they were in reality a mixture of memory and improvisation.

Then came the sermon, which went on for a long time. Molly and Thomas usually withdrew their attention during the sermon, for it was invariably devoted to harangues against laziness, dirtiness, bickering, impurity of thought, and lack of respect by the young toward their elders and by everyone toward the Reader himself. This week everybody was listening, in hope that something would be said about the incomers. But William Jonas, aware of an audience which for once was hanging on his words, took the opportunity to sermonize for even longer than usual, and to give various of his complaints an especially thorough airing. It wasn't until the very end of the service, after the last hymn, that the Reader announced a meeting of all adult islanders, in the same place after dinner, to decide on a matter of the highest importance to them all. And from this announcement he modulated into the benediction:

'And, Deliverer, guide us with your wisdom and help us to do that which is right and to defeat the Bad One and all his works, and keep us safe from sin on this blessed isle, and long may we live and prosper and be a credit to your name and memory. And so say all of us.'

43

'And so say all of us!' echoed the congregation thankfully. Then the villagers made their way out into the sunshine as quickly as they could without unseemly jostling.

The boat party had still not returned. But two or three people had climbed to the high point just outside the village known as the Lookout; and there was hardly time for gossip to get under way in the open space in front of the Meeting-House before somebody shouted 'Here they come!' And soon the villagers could all see the island boat, with its sail up, coming into view from behind the headland, and running at a fair speed towards the landing-place with a favourable wind behind it.

A few of the men, and all the children, scrambled down the steep track to the landing. The boat dropped its sail, and Jacob Wilde steered it expertly past the reef, between the rocks, and into the tiny inlet. Men leaped out and drew it up on to the sand.

The clumsy, clinker-built boat was full. Besides its crew of six it was carrying old Abel and the two incomers. The girl and boy in turn were picked up and passed to islanders ashore. Both were obviously still weak. Someone lifted Mua on to the broad back of Alec Campbell, while Bob Attwood took Otipo. Without any sign of effort they led the procession up the track. Abel, looking anxious, but almost as agile as a young man, followed closely behind.

On the grassy plain, they were surrounded by the remaining islanders and made their way in a moving circle toward the Meeting-House. In front of it was a bench on which the incomers were put down gently, side by side. Each had on a sheepskin jacket and a mixture of items from Abel's decrepit wardrobe. The clothing didn't disguise the fact that they were still pathetically thin, and several of their sores and bruises could be seen. The girl shivered; the boy put out a hand to take hers and smiled at her; she smiled faintly back.

And Molly, standing among the crowd, felt a wave of sympathy run round it. Women murmured 'Poor souls!' and 'Only young!' Some of the men and children went up to the incomers and asked them in loud voices, as if that would help them to understand, who they were and where they came from. Others waited hopefully for them to say something in their own language, for no islander until now had heard a foreign tongue being used. But the pair, looking apprehensive, made no reply until at length the boy drew himself up and declared with dignity, 'Issawright.'

The Reader was not there; obviously he hadn't seen fit to dignify this occasion with his presence. Jacob Wilde, a stolid man of about fifty, was the most important person present. He scratched his head, uncertain what to do next. Then Abby Jonas, little-girlish in her Prayer-Day muslin dress with a blue sash, came tripping down from the Reader's house. A way was cleared for her, and she whispered, with a hand to her mouth and a great show of confidentiality, into Jacob's ear.

'Huh! She makes a lot of to-do about it!' snorted Molly; but Thomas only grinned. Jacob's face cleared.

'Well, that's settled,' he announced. 'These two are to have their dinner at my house. And, just to make matters clear, that don't mean nothing. It don't mean they'll be accepted on Halcyon. Afterwards Luke'll ring the bell, and all that's entitled to attend will come to the Meeting-House.' And he added, speaking to Dick Reeves as the people began to drift away, 'Your Thomas and Molly are to come to the meeting as well, and my Dan. The Reader wants them to tell everyone what happened.'

Molly and Thomas had the midday dinner of fish and potatoes alone with their parents. Adam and Beth, who would normally have been there, were absent.

'They're going round the village talking to folk,' Dick Reeves said, 'trying to persuade them the incomers should stay.' He sounded dubious. 'I don't know what the Reader'll say about that.'

'There's nothing in the Book to prevent it, is there?' asked Hester.

'You don't know *what* might be in the Book,' said Dick. 'The Reader might know something we don't. He's very well acquainted with the Book, is William Jonas. A knowledgeable man. Very thorough. He could hardly know more if he'd spelt it out for himself.'

Dick shook his head.

'I don't like our Beth, or Adam, putting themselves forward like that,' he went on. 'It don't do them any good, you know. They should leave that kind of thing to the older folk and them that's in charge, like the Reader and Jacob Wilde. Lie low and keep out of trouble, that's what *I* say.'

Dick Reeves dozed for a while after dinner. Prayer Day was his one day without work, and he appreciated it. But before long the Calling Bell was heard. Luke Jonas rang it with extra and prolonged vigour, to mark the importance of the occasion, and grinned more broadly than ever as people streamed past him into the Meeting-House. Molly and Thomas, still stiff and awkward in their best clothes, caught something of this sense of occasion, and felt at the same time important and nervous.

The Reader stood at the lectern, with the Book open in front of him. He was wearing a full-length red dressing-gown, brought out only for special events, and looked very impressive. He made signs to the young people to come and sit on the bench immediately in front of him, which already held Dan Wilde and Jemmy Kane. A minute later, Otipo and Mua were also directed to this bench. Otipo put out both hands toward Thomas and Molly, but the Reader sternly motioned him back.

The Meeting-House filled up. Even old Uncle Ben Attwood, who considered himself too feeble to go to the weekly service, and Aunt Susan Campbell, who was supposed to be bedridden, had managed to hobble along. Luke Jonas stopped ringing the bell, came inside, and sat on the upturned box which served as his seat, just inside the door.

The Reader raised both arms, as a signal to everyone to stand.

'We will begin our proceedings with a prayer to the Deliverer,' he announced, and extemporised a long and somewhat muddled prayer in which he asked for help in arriving at whatever decision the Deliverer in his wisdom had decided they should arrive at.

'And now,' he said, 'Thomas Reeves, step forward.'

Thomas got up and stood before him. There was a rustle of interest.

'Answer me, Thomas, with truth in your soul,' the Reader said. 'I understand that you were the first to see the boat that brought these incomers to our shore.'

'No, sir, that was Molly.'

'But you led the way down to rescue them?'

'I suppose so.'

'Thomas, tell the people all about it.'

Thomas described the rescue in detail. When he had finished, the Reader asked him,

'Did you, Thomas, at any time, see any other figure in that boat?'

Thomas stared.

'What sort of figure?' he asked.

'A figure that might have looked human, or might have been like a shadow or a ghost?'

'You mean . . .'

'You know what I mean!' said the Reader grimly.

'No, sir,' said Thomas firmly, 'I did not.' And when Molly was called in turn to testify, she was asked the same question and gave the same answer. But when Dan was asked, he didn't seem quite so sure.

'I thought at first, looking from the cliff, there was three people in the boat,' he said. 'But when we got there, there was only two.'

'So,' said the Reader. 'At one time there was three figures in the boat. Listen well to that, brothers and sisters.'

'No, I didn't say there *was* three,' said Dan uneasily. 'I just thought for a while there might be. But I was a long way away.'

'And when you dragged the boat over the reef,' the Reader said. 'Then what did you think?'

'Well, like I told my dad, I didn't think we could get it over, we wasn't strong enough. And then, all of a sudden, it lifted, like as if someone was helping us, and over it came.'

'It was a big wave,' said Thomas, interrupting.

'That'll do, Thomas Reeves,' the Reader told him sternly. 'You've given your evidence. There's no more to come from you.'

'It might have been a big wave,' Dan agreed.

'And it might not!' said the Reader darkly. 'You can sit down, Daniel. Now, Jeremiah Kane!'

Jemmy Kane stepped forward eagerly.

'Luke,' the Reader ordered. 'Bring a box for this child to stand on, that the people may see and hear him.'

Luke had sat in a state of bafflement through the proceedings, which seemed to be beyond his comprehension. But he could understand that. He got up from the box on which he was sitting, and dragged it across the floor. Then he lifted Jemmy and stood him on it, in full view of the gathering. Jemmy smirked, obviously enjoying his prominence.

'Answer me, Jeremiah, with truth in your soul,' the Reader told him.

'Look at that gleam in his eye. There ain't no truth in *his* soul!' Molly muttered to Thomas.

'Be quiet, Molly Reeves!' the Reader instructed her. 'Now, Jeremiah, you too were on the cliff gathering eggs when the boat came into view?'

'Yes, sir.' Jemmy's voice was clear and penetrating.

'And how many people did you think were in it?'

'Three, sir. There was definitely three. If you count them all as people.'

A startled whisper ran round the gathering. The Reader continued.

'You climbed down the cliff as fast as you could. When you got to the bottom, what did you see?'

'I saw Molly and Thomas, what was trying to get out to the boat.'

'And the boat itself. Did it still seem to have three figures in it?'

'Yes, sir.'

'Were the two young people you see in front of you among them?'

'Yes, sir.'

'And what was the third?'

'It was a sort of black thing.'

'A person?'

'A bit like a person. But it looked real bad and ugly. I thought it was the Bad One.'

'There wasn't any such thing!' Molly called out.

'Be quiet!' the Reader told her for the second time.

'But there wasn't!' Thomas shouted, indignant. 'There was just them, Otipo and Mua, all the time!'

'You be quiet, too, Thomas! I'm warning you!'

Molly nudged Dan Wilde, who was sitting at the other side of her from Thomas.

'Go on!' she urged him in a fierce whisper. 'Tell him! There wasn't no black thing! Jemmy's making it all up!'

But Dan sat silent and uncomfortable, as if unsure what he had and hadn't seen.

'Let the child continue!' the Reader said. 'Jeremiah, you now swam out to the canoe, to help bring it in. Is that right?'

'Yes, sir.'

'Was this third figure still in the boat?'

'No, sir. I reckon it had got out.'

'It had vanished?'

'No, sir. I reckon it had got out an' was pushing from behind.'

Adam Goodall strode forward from the middle of the gathering.

'Sir, this is ridiculous!' he objected. 'You can't take any notice of this kind of nonsense!'

'Adam Goodall,' said William, 'you're not the Reader. I am. And it's me that's running this inquiry. So in the name of the Deliverer, sit down and close your mouth! Now, Jeremiah, did you see any more of this black figure?'

'No, sir,' said Jemmy.

'By the time you got the boat ashore, it had gone?'

'Yes, sir.'

'Done its work!' called Sarah Jonas from amid the audience.

'Rubbish!' shouted Adam angrily.

'I told you to shut up, Adam Goodall! Jeremiah, you can get down from that box. Let the incomers themselves stand before me!'

The boy and girl were pushed forward. Otipo stood up steadily, though uncomprehending. But Mua was still hardly able to stand. Molly darted forward from the front bench and seated her on the box that Jemmy had just left.

'Yes, she can sit down,' said the Reader, regularizing the position.

'Do you understand me?' he asked Otipo in a loud voice.

Otipo stared.

'Do you know any English?'

Otipo still stared. Then he said, uncertainly, 'Issawright.'

'That ain't no answer,' said the Reader. Then, 'Do you have knowledge of the Bad One?'

No reply.

'If you have no knowledge of the Bad One, say "No" or shake your head.'

Still no reply.

'That's not fair!' Thomas broke out. 'He doesn't understand you!'

'Maybe not,' said the Reader. 'Or maybe he understands me but he won't admit it. Anyway, I've told you already, young Thomas, you sit down and hold your peace!' Then he called loudly, 'You, the Bad One! I order you in the name of the Deliverer! If you are in one of these two, come out and declare yourself!'

Nothing happened. The Reader now seemed at a loss.

'I can't see that I'm going to get anything out of them,' he said at length. 'They might as well go back to their seats.' And when Otipo and Mua, their faces still blank, had been led away, he went on,

'Jacob Wilde!'

Dan's father described briefly how he had helmed the boat that went round the headland to pick up the incomers. No, he had not been able to communicate with them. No, he had not seen any mysterious figures. Yes, he had heard what Jemmy Kane said. Did he think Jemmy was telling the truth? He couldn't say.

'And about this boat they came in, Jacob?' the Reader asked. 'This canoe or whatever it is?'

'Oh, *that!*' said Jacob, seeming more at ease with the subject of boats than with that of the Bad One. 'We didn't think much of it. Just a light frame job, covered with bark or some such. No good for the seas we have around here.'

'And you left it where it was, Jacob?'

'Yes, it's stove in. It ain't no use to us, even if we could repair it. And some of the lads didn't like to handle it.'

'Now that's interesting,' the Reader said. 'Here's a boat that ain't fit for our seas, and yet it arrives here, having apparently — I say apparently — come an enormous distance. I must say, that seems uncanny to me. Suspicious, to say the least . . . All right, Jacob, if you've nothing more to say you can sit down. I reckon that's all the evidence we're going to get.'

'Hey, what about me?' demanded Abel.

The Reader was angry.

'You ain't been called, Abel Oakes!' he said. 'And I've had enough interruptions. You keep quiet or I'll have you thrown out of here, old as you are!'

There was old antagonism between Abel and the Reader. Abel flared up.

'I'm the same age as you are, William Jonas,' he declared. 'Or within a year or two. And a better man than you any day. Always was and still am.' He shook a bony fist.

Luke moved across from the doorway, grinning happily at the thought of action.

'Keep your hands off Uncle Abel, Luke!' ordered Adam.

'I should let Abel have his say if I was you, Reader,' said Jacob Wilde quietly. And the Reader gave way.

'All right, Abel,' he said. 'I ought to know by now, it's no good expecting you to behave proper. Tell the people what you have to say.'

'I don't have much to say,' Abel began. 'Only that I've had the care of them these last few days, and I reckon they're just a couple of children, like they might have been mine if I'd been luckier, and like they might be anybody else's. And I didn't see nothing of the Bad One, nor ever have done for that matter, all my life. And I think they've come a long way over the sea, and it's a miracle that they're still alive, and I reckon they should stay so. And I say we don't give nobody back to the sea that's escaped from it, and if anybody's to be drowned I'd sooner it was me than them. Just look at their innocent faces! You see any evil there? Course you don't! It's all a lot of nonsense, William Jonas, and at your age you should know better!'

William was impressed in spite of himself.

'It's not me, it's the Book,' he said defensively. 'We're told to cast out evil, and it's up to me as Reader to see we do. There ain't no malice about it. And now, Abel Oakes, you've had your say and so has everyone else that knows anything about this, and it's my turn next. And it seems to me that we can't be too careful.'

He went to the Book and turned a few pages over at random, by way of claiming its authority for what he was going to say. Then he repeated from memory the Teaching handed down to him by previous Readers.

'So you see,' he concluded, 'we have to have a meeting of the people, but it seems to me the Book tells them what they have to do. It was done twice in my father's day and three or four times in my grandpa's. And I heard about all them cases from my dad's own lips, and I reckon none of them was as strong as this one, because nobody in them other cases actually saw the Bad One.'

'You don't believe Jemmy's rubbish, do you?' demanded Adam.

'That's one interruption too many!' said the Reader. 'Take him away, Luke!'

Luke looked warily at Adam, who was taller and more strongly built than he was himself, and shook his head. The Reader decided not to press the matter, and went on.

'It says elsewhere in the Teaching, "From the mouths of infants shall the truth proceed when they that are full grown know it not." Now it seems to me that this could be a time the Deliverer had in mind. But in any case, it don't depend on what Jemmy saw. We know from the Book that shipwreck is the wages of sin, and we know what we have to do. So I say, we've talked about it enough, and it's time to come to a decision!'

'May I speak, Reader?' asked Hester Reeves, standing up in her place just behind Molly and Thomas.

The Reader looked as if he'd have liked to say 'No,' but Hester was respected in the village.

'All right,' he said. 'Don't be too long about it.'

'Friends,' said Hester, 'you've all seen the two incomers, and it seems to me you'll all agree with Uncle Abel, they're no more than children, no older than my Molly and Thomas, if as old. I don't believe that children can form an evil intent.'

'The Bad One might work through anybody!' the Reader said. 'And why not children? Just the sort of cunning thing he'd do!'

'As for Jemmy,' said Hester, 'I seem to remember he said he hadn't seen Maggie Campbell's apples, but they was found in his sleeping-place, and then he admitted he'd took 'em. So I don't put too much belief in his black creature!'

'He's the biggest little liar on the island!' Molly added hotly.

There were murmurs of apparent agreement.

The Reader was getting weary now.

'I've had enough of all this,' he said. 'Argue, argue, argue. Interrupt, interrupt, interrupt. No respect. Well, I done my duty. I told you what the Book says and what I think you should do. Now I'm going to take a vote. Will all them that agrees we should act according to the Book, and cast out the incomers from among us and remain in the ways of righteousness, hold up their right hand and be counted?'

A few hands went up, then a few more.

'Seth Attwood!' the Reader called. 'I don't see your hand up!'

'I ain't sure that I agree,' said Seth from the third row back.

'Well, make up your mind quickly. Aunt Annie Jonas, I don't see your hand up, neither, in spite of all that rhubarb you had off my plot last year.'

Reluctantly, Annie put up her hand. But when the Reader asked sharp-tongued Martha Goodall, Adam's mother, she said, 'No, I ain't voted for you and I'm not going to, either!'

'That'll do, William,' said old Abel. 'You're supposed to be taking a vote, not telling people what to do. Get counting!'

Another two or three hands had been raised by now. William and Abel counted them together. Twenty-eight votes, mostly those of the older and more rigid-minded islanders, were cast in favour of rejecting the incomers. But when the Reader called for votes against, twice as many hands went up.

A ripple of hesitant applause ran round the Meeting-House. Molly put an arm round Mua and kissed her.

'All right,' the Reader said disapprovingly. 'You've most of you voted to give the Bad One his chance. All I can say is, watch out for what he does next, and if you don't like it, don't blame me!'

'May I ask what becomes of these youngsters now?' inquired Jacob Wilde.

'They'll stay with me, of course!' declared Abel. He put his wiry arms protectively round Otipo and Mua, who were both smiling. Though they hadn't understood the proceedings, it was clear that they knew the outcome was favourable.

'And how are you going to feed them, Abel?' asked Jacob. 'They won't be fit to work for a while, you know. And they probably ain't used to our kind of work anyway.'

'I don't care if they never work!' Abel said. 'I got my children at last!'

'Very well, Abel,' said the Reader. He turned and addressed the gathering.

'It is decided that the incomers can stay. And as Reader and Guardian of the Book, I rule that Abel Oakes shall maintain them, and on his own head be it. And I advise all folk that have any sense to steer well clear of them, so as not to risk their immortal souls.'

'And the boat?' asked Jacob Wilde.

'The boat can stay where it is. Most likely it's contaminated with evil. Anyway, it doesn't sound as if it'd be any good to us. Right, that's everything settled, isn't it? I declare the meeting closed, and high time too.'

'If only my Jess could have seen this day!' said Abel, beaming, on the way out. 'The happiest since she died!'

The Reader shook his head.

'Oh, Abel, Abel!' he said solemnly. 'Little do you know what harm your pigheadedness may bring to us all!'

'Pigheaded yourself!' retorted Abel with relish.

The Reeves family, returning with Adam to their own house, found the way temporarily blocked by thin, narrow-faced Harry Kane, who was a widower and Jemmy's father, and hefty Bob Attwood, notorious for his bad temper.

'You needn't think because I didn't interrupt I didn't hear you!' Harry told the Reeveses. '*And* you, Adam Goodall. You all been calling my Jemmy a liar!'

'He *is* a liar,' said Thomas.

'Quiet, Thomas!' said Adam sharply. 'Don't provoke them!'

Bob Attwood, scowling, had clenched a massive fist. He seemed on the point of hitting Thomas. Harry Kane put a hand on his friend's shoulder.

'Not now, Bob,' he said. 'I'm just warning them, that's all. I won't have my lad talked about like that. Let me remind all concerned that Jemmy, like me, is a descendant of the Deliverer, no less. Anyone that attacks our good name will have to answer to me for it!'

'And me!' growled Bob. 'Harry's me pal and Jemmy's me pal's son, and I'll stand by them.'

'May we come past, please?' asked Hester Reeves calmly.

'Course you may,' said Harry. 'I've said what I had to say. Remember it, that's all.'

'I haven't noticed Harry caring much about young Jemmy before,' Hester remarked as the Reeveses went with Adam into their own house.

'He's peeved because it all happened in public,' Adam said. 'But Harry's not a fighter, and Bob follows his lead. I don't think we need worry about them.'

Dick Reeves wasn't so sure.

'You shouldn't have said what you did, none of you!' he told his family. 'No good ever comes of putting people's backs up. It may turn out you been doing the Bad One's work, stirring up trouble. Ever thought of that, eh? Ever thought of that?'

Second Wave

DAYS *lengthen and grow warmer. Winds slacken from fierce to moderate and sometimes light, though a day without any wind at all is unknown on Halcyon. Sky and sea are mainly blue, and on many a day the only cloud to be seen is the circlet surrounding the head of the Peak. Kingfisher rides peacefully on the horizon, as if at anchor.*

In sheltered spots around Halcyon, a few stunted apple and cherry trees struggle into bloom. Sheep-shearing comes, and the men and dogs round up the rams and ewes, dip them in the Dam, clip their heavy fleeces and send them back to the mountainside. Spinning-wheels are moved out to cottage doorways.

This is the time of plenty. There are no more seabirds' eggs, for those the islanders didn't take have all hatched out now; but the young birds can be caught and eaten, and the island hens are laying well. The fishing is good, and less perilous now than it is at other times of year. There's a lot of work to be done in the vegetable plots, but the islanders don't mind that. 'Better hard work and full belly than sit and starve' is an old Halcyon saying. Apart from a handful of unsatisfactory folk like Harry Kane and Bob Attwood and Bob's wife Lazy Lucy, the islanders believe in this saying and act on it. They would rather work out of doors from dawn to dusk than endure the endless successions of winter days when vile weather keeps them idle and hungry at home.

Excitement over the incomers has died down. Abel Oakes has kept them tactfully away from the village; and the islanders have obeyed the Reader's instruction to avoid them. Truth to tell, most people are a little afraid, and not entirely sure that the Bad One is not in some way involved. Everyone is busy, and there are plenty of other things to think about, though nobody forgets that Otipo and Mua are there.

Yet fears diminish as time goes by and no apparent harm comes to the island. No one is drowned or falls from the cliffs; no one is ill except an old uncle and a couple of aunties who are in their late eighties and nearing their final rest. The sheep show no signs of scab and the lambs are healthy. The early potatoes and root vegetables are coming on well. No islander will go hungry to bed in the next few weeks. It is time for the yearly celebration: for Lifting Day and the Dance.

Chapter 5

'Got any old clothes, Moll?' Thomas asked.

'What do you mean, have I any old clothes? I got nothing *but* old clothes,' Molly said tartly.

'You know what I mean. Anything you've stopped wearing.'

'Not much. You know where my things go. They're passed on to Sally Goodall.' And then, suspiciously, 'What do you want them for, anyway?'

Thomas hesitated.

'Well . . .'

'All right, you don't need to tell me. It's for that girl, isn't it?'

'Well . . .'

'She's only half my size,' Molly said. 'Why don't you ask Abby Jonas?'

'Some hope!' said Thomas. He mimicked Abby's tone of voice. '"I must ask my grandpa first!" That's what she'd say. I wouldn't get anything from the Jonases. Come on, Moll, see what you can find!'

'I'll have a look,' said Molly. And then, her voice rising in exasperation, 'It's not fair, Thomas Reeves! When we was children we was treated equal, and now look at the way it is! Specially since the incomers came! You can go where you like; you only have to say you're off to the sheep or the vegetable plots and there's no questions asked. And *I* know where you've been going lately. As for me, I might as well be an ox in a stall for all the freedom I have!'

'What's that?' demanded Hester Reeves, coming in with a pail of milk from the goat. 'Complaining again, are you, my girl? And shouting at your brother!'

'What if I am?' said Molly sullenly. 'I'm sick of being at home, and watched all the time.'

'It won't get you nowhere,' said Hester. 'There's too many lined up against you, Molly Reeves. And it mostly comes from having too much to say. The Reader didn't like it in Thomas, and he liked it still less in a girl. And what with him saying you was getting out of hand, and your dad agreeing with him, and Jacob Wilde telling them he might ask for you for Dan if only you'd behave yourself . . . No wonder they all said it was time you learned to stay in the house and act like a woman. And then the Reader thinking you and Abby ought to be friends . . .'

'That's the worst bit of all!' said Molly. 'I can't abide that Abby Jonas. And I reckon she spies on me. I can't move an inch or say a word out of turn without it comes back to me from you or Dad, by way of the Reader. It ain't fair!' She was close to tears.

'There, there,' said Hester. 'It's not that I ain't sympathetic. I am, Molly. I can remember feeling just like you do now. But that's how life is on Halcyon. I don't know any way you can stop yourself being a woman. As for you, Thomas, you needn't think I don't know what you're up to. Two or three times a week you've been down at Abel's cave, haven't you?'

'What if I have?'

'Well, *I* don't mind. I ain't lost interest in the incomers since I stopped needing to go and nurse them. I don't see no harm in them. But you know what orders the Reader gave. You'll get yourself into trouble if you're caught, and maybe me and your dad, too. And what's the attraction?'

'I expect he fancies that girl!' said Molly jealously.

Thomas didn't react to the remark.

'I like to be with them,' he said calmly. 'They're interesting. Not like Halcyon folk at all.'

'It's just because they're new, I expect,' said Hester.

'Well, maybe. I don't know. But I'm learning their language and teaching them ours, and it's fun.'

'Sounds more like hard work to me,' said Hester.

'They're very clever. They learn fast. And they do all sorts of things. They *sing*.'

'Well, *we* sing,' said Molly. 'In the Meeting-House on Prayer Day.'

'Theirs is a different kind of singing. Very strange. I don't really understand it. Sort of quiet, and answering each other's voices. When they tell me what the songs mean, I still don't understand, but the singing does something to me. And they tell stories.'

'Stories is sinful, according to the Teaching.'

'The Teaching ain't everything,' said Thomas.

'Well you be careful what you say about it,' Hester advised him.

'And they dance. Not like we do, clomping around. It's as if it was saying something, the way the songs and stories are saying something, but a different language . . . And they carve. Abel finds bits of wood for them and lends them his knife. They carve figures.'

'What sort of figures?' asked Molly.

'Birds and fishes, mostly. And dolphins. And people, sometimes. Naked people.'

'*Naked* people?' Hester and Molly were round-eyed with shocked surprise.

'And boats,' Thomas added, hastily moving on. 'They carve little tiny boats, like the one they came in.'

'Talking of boats,' Hester said, 'Adam told me he was over the other side of the headland a few days ago and he saw that boat sailing, inside the reef.'

'Yes, well, he may have done. It's been mended. Abel's good at boats. He found some timber and sailcloth, and they worked out a way to repair it.'

'Abel seems to have all sorts of things!' remarked Hester. 'Timber's scarce, and so is sailcloth. But I suppose he's been hoarding things for years. Well, if I was him or you, I'd remember that boats is visible, and liable to attract attention.'

'You're not really against us, are you, Mum?' said Thomas with some relief.

'No, I'm not against you. But I'm telling you again, be careful.'

'Abel has a plan,' said Thomas. 'He thinks enough time's gone by for him to introduce Otipo and Mua at the village. And he's chosen his occasion.'

'When will it be?'

'I promised not to tell,' said Thomas. 'But it'll surprise you. It'll surprise everybody. It'll be something you'll never forget.'

'So that's why you want clothes?' Molly asked.

'Yes. Mua needs something fit to wear in public. She can't go around for ever wrapped in stinking old sheepskins.'

'Clothes aren't laid by the birds, you know,' said Hester.

'I got a few things,' said Molly. 'There was that skirt and petticoat that I grew out of. And the vest you thought I might wear again some time, but I never did. And a pair of white wool stockings.'

'And what will we hand on to Sally Goodall?' her mother asked.

'Well, with you and me and Beth in the house, we'll find something,' Molly said. And then, with a touch of defiance, 'I'm going with Thomas to take the things to Abel's.'

But that was too much.

'Oh no, you're not!' her mother declared. 'Your dad'll be back from the fishing any time now. He'd take the strap to you when you came in. And anyway, I forbid it.'

'One of these days,' said Molly, 'I'll just go, and it'll be too late to do anything about it.'

'I'll give you a bit of advice,' said Hester Reeves thoughtfully. 'Save your defiance for a time when you really need it. You may only have one chance, so don't use it too soon. And now, Thomas, take the stuff and get out, and remember, I don't know nothing about it.'

'Thanks, Mum,' Thomas said. Molly watched ruefully when, five minutes later, he left the cottage with her old clothes tucked under his arm.

'You'll just have to realize,' her mother told her, 'that things is different for boys. You're headstrong, Molly, that's what you are. I don't wonder your dad says you're more like a real lad than Thomas. But it won't do. You're a woman already, almost. Just look at the size and shape of you. If you don't settle down to it, I don't know how you'll ever get a husband. If *I* was Dan Wilde, I wouldn't be so keen to take you on.'

'I don't care for Dan Wilde,' said Molly.

'If I was *any* young man, I'd think twice before I'd wed a firebrand like you,' Hester said. She paused and reflected.

'Not that I'd want you different, exactly,' she said. 'Come here, love, and let me kiss you.'

The procession wound its way up the track which led across the upland to the vegetable plots, a couple of miles from the village. The Reader was first, sitting with Sarah Jonas beside him in an ox-cart drawn by a pair of yoked beasts. Slow-witted Luke, who loved all such occasions, walked alongside, brandishing a switch and grinning broadly all the time.

Next came a second ox-cart carrying Jacob Wilde, the Senior Elder. Beside him sat his wife Rebecca, enjoying the occasion as much as Luke and nodding graciously from time to time, while Dan led the oxen. Behind them rode such of the other island men as owned donkeys. The men who didn't own donkeys straggled behind on foot. Then came the women, and finally the children. Everyone wore Prayer-Day best. The children were in new knitted clothes or newly handed-down old ones. Those who had boots wore them; the rest wore ox-hide or sheepskin moccasins. It wasn't proper to go barefoot on Lifting Day.

Eventually the procession arrived at the vegetable plots. The Reader walked solemnly around them, inspecting the growing plants and bending down once or twice to remove a caterpillar or to pick a leaf between thumb and forefinger and examine it expertly. He arrived, last of all, at the early potatoes. The growth above ground was fine and healthy, and the rows had been earthed up in beautiful straight lines. Not a weed was to be seen.

'Very good,' the Reader said. 'Very good indeed. A credit to all concerned.' He motioned to Luke to come forward. Luke was now carrying the island's best garden fork, ordered from the mainland many years ago, when ships still called at Halcyon.

'I am ready,' the Reader announced. 'Hand me the implement.'

He took the fork, plunged it into the soil and drew the tines upward. A dozen or more small white potatoes, precious nuggets of food, were uncovered and raised to the surface. A sigh of relief went up from the islanders, followed by a round of applause. The Reader bowed.

'Let us thank the Deliverer,' he said solemnly, 'for bestowing upon us these first-fruits of the year's crop. Let us ask him to bless not only the earlies but also the second earlies and the main crop. And let us beg that all our other crops shall thrive equally, including the beans that didn't do too well last year, and that the autumn and winter be mild and the people prosper. And' – he turned and spoke loudly and sternly to those behind him – 'let us by our behaviour merit the treatment we hope to receive. And that includes you, Harry Kane, and you, Bob Attwood, and all you children that are fooling around over there. For assuredly, if we sink into sin and do the things we ought not to do, the Deliverer will turn away from us, and we shall get the punishment we deserve!'

A shudder ran through the gathering.

'And now,' the Reader went on, 'I declare that today is to be a day of joy and holiday, a day of hope and thanksgiving and good resolutions. And a lovely day it is, I must say, and let's give the Deliverer extra thanks for matching it to the occasion. And let no more work be done until sun-up tomorrow. And so say all of us.'

'And so say all of us!' came the response. A thin cheer went up from the children at the back of the gathering. With great dignity the Reader clambered on to his ox-cart, and the procession re-formed. It made its way back to the village, with a slight detour to take in the Lookout, a high point from

64

which it was said the Deliverer had surveyed the island on first arrival and found it good.

Here there was a pause while the Reader said a few suitable words. And, to Molly and Thomas, Halcyon did indeed look good: southward the Peak; westward the Sound, with the hazy violet-grey hump of Kingfisher far out on the horizon; to north and east the upland, with its new bright grass and sheep and yellow gorse, sloping down to the grey stone walls of the village; and beyond all that for ever and ever the blue infinity of sea and sky.

At the Meeting-House, the Lifting Day banquet had already been prepared. There was crayfish to start with; then the main course of roast mutton, stuffed with onion and mashed potato and celery, with baked and boiled potatoes on the side. The meat was carefully apportioned, according to the size and standing of the islander who received it; but there was unlimited potato, for the old crop had lasted out. After that there was cranberry pudding, made with cranberries from the marshland at the mouth of Big Gulch; and as a final treat for adults only there was tea, made from a small cache which Uncle Ben Attwood had been cherishing ever since the schooner *Arabella* called at Halcyon six years earlier.

Then came half an hour's rest, for sitting in stupefied silence after unaccustomed over-eating, and exchanging small-talk about the welfare of people, animals and crops. This was the Social, and was followed by the long afternoon thanksgiving service. And then the Reader and Sarah Jonas and the elders went home, and the Dance began.

Strictly speaking, the Dance was not approved of. At each year's Council of Elders, the Reader proposed that it should be stopped. It was not in keeping, he felt, with the standards of righteousness that the Deliverer would have wished the islanders to observe. Dancing was enjoyable, and therefore probably sinful, though he had to admit that the Teaching as handed down did not forbid it.

Somehow each discussion ended with reluctant agreement that the Dance could continue for the time being. The younger islanders expected and looked forward to it, and might well get up to even more sinful activities if it were ended. The elders took the precaution of patrolling the Dell, where most of the struggling apple trees grew, and where courting couples had been known to wander.

So, when the older people had gone home, the younger ones began the Dance, to the strains of Sam Goodall's fiddle, which didn't seem to perform any the worse for having only three strings. Islanders pounded vigorously around the Meeting-House in jigs, reels, and a variety of traditional dances. The climax and conclusion was the Potato Dance, in which an outsize specimen of that vegetable was thrown by a man to a woman of his choice, and then by her to another man, and so on, with each recipient in turn holding high the potato and leading a growing line of dancers as they capered around the room. Anyone who dropped the potato was out, and was heartily jeered at; but this was a rare occurrence, for the islanders were sure-footed and sure-fingered. Molly found herself halfway down the line, having received the potato by way of a difficult catch from Dan Wilde and disposed of it by a gentle one offered to Thomas, who always feared disgrace.

The person who finally headed the line was Beth's Adam. The room was hot by now, and the dancers all perspiring; and Adam led the chain out through the Meeting-House door into the cool air of the long light midsummer evening. And, once in the open, the chain broke up in astonishment. For in the grassy open space outside the Meeting-House was Uncle Abel; and, one on each side of him, their arms linked with his, were Otipo and Mua.

They were fully recovered now from their ordeal; and in spite of the weird mixtures of cast-off island clothes that they were wearing, their appearance stirred admiration and a tinge of envy in the younger islanders, for their figures were slim and erect, their oval faces smooth, their eyes clear and bright. Chattering died down and everyone stood looking at them in silence.

'These are my two,' announced Abel proudly; and then, 'Where's William Jonas?'

'Gone home.'

'And Jacob Wilde?'

'Gone home, too.'

'There's none of the elders around?'

'No, Abel. They never stay for the Dance.'

'Then there ain't nobody to give me permission, is there?' said Abel. 'Nor to deny it me, neither!' He beamed. 'You been having the Dance, ain't you? For Lifting Day? I know about the Dance, I jumped around in it plenty in my young days. But now let me tell you, you don't know nothing about dancing. I got somebody here that can show you. My children!'

'My grandpa told us not to associate with them,' said Abby Jonas primly.

'You don't have to associate, me dear,' said Abel. 'Just watch, like everybody else. My two wasn't so sure they wanted to do it at first, but I persuaded them.' He unlinked himself from Otipo and Mua.

'Now!' he said. 'You show them! Dance!'

Otipo smiled.

'We shall dance,' he said clearly; and then, 'But I cannot dance like this.' And he began pulling off the motley garments in which Abel had arrayed him.

The watchers gasped, and Abel, alarmed, exhorted him, 'Careful, lad. That's enough.'

To the relief of the modest islanders, Otipo halted the process when he had reduced what he was wearing to a pair of gray and ragged underpants. Molly was embarrassed; it seemed to her that this was far too little for a young man to have on; but she couldn't help contrasting the lean and neatly-muscled Otipo with skinny Thomas and beefy oxlike Dan.

Otipo dropped to the ground and lay flat on his back, all in one movement; it looked for a moment as if he had fallen dead. Only his eyes moved at first. Then his fingers stirred and rippled; his arms moved in parallel, describing arcs from the ground beyond his head to beside his thighs and back again. The arcs shifted and changed, while always mirroring each other; the hands with their fluttering fingers swam through the air; then, as if the flying fingers were raising it from the ground, the upper part of his body rose and began to move, backward and forward, round and round. He was seated now, and the movements of body, arms, hands and fingers wove a complex, continually-changing pattern, slow at first, then swifter and swifter.

Then Otipo was upright, with legs and feet joining in the rapid pattern of movement: leaping, spinning, stopping suddenly and reversing the spin, but always staying on the same spot while the hands and ever-busy fingers climbed up and down or swung around. Mua was now clapping her hands inaudibly together as if timing the dance: faster and faster, until with a final whirlwind flourish Otipo brought every movement to a halt and dropped on his knees in front of her.

The islanders stood dazed. There was hardly time for a ragged round of applause to begin before Mua was moving. She too wriggled from the thick woollen clothing like a bird escaping from a cage, until there was only a slight garment round her hips, not of island origin at all. There were more gasps, but the islanders were awestruck rather than shocked. Mua began to dance: slowly, slowly, with an unsmiling solemnity, arms curving and torso swaying; fingers weaving in quick, light counterpoint.

As her movements grew swifter she freed herself from the spot, dipping and wheeling with extended arms, and making little high mewing sounds like a seabird. And at last Otipo lifted her and she was on his shoulders, and they were circling together in a miracle of balance, and they were slowing, slowing, with Mua's arms still outspread, until suddenly she was down and they had stopped, silent and motionless, facing each other. The islanders around them were equally silent, the impact too great for applause.

Abel began desperately to heap clothes upon them. They didn't resist as the heavy ugliness of island garments descended on them, giving a kind of invisibility, so that in a moment the almost-naked bodies of the dance seemed like a vanished illusion.

Molly turned to Thomas, still next to her from the Potato Dance.

'That,' she said, 'was the most beautiful thing I ever saw.'

Thomas wasn't listening. His eyes were on Mua's face. And Molly saw that tears were running down the girl's cheeks.

Islanders had gathered around but were keeping a respectful, astonished distance. Thomas asked Otipo, 'Why is she crying?'

'She is sad,' Otipo said. 'It is dance we do for our own people. Now we have no people. Other time we have island like this; is called Rikofia. We have Peak like this. Then . . .'

He made gestures with his arms.

'He means it blew up,' said Abel. 'Erupted. Like ours might do, some day.'

'Yes,' said Otipo. 'It erupt. Some people die, some people go away in boats. But we not see them again. I think they all drown. I think only I and Mua alive now.'

'Oh, you poor things!' cried Molly, putting her arms round Mua.

There were tears in Thomas's eyes; he had been moved first by the dance and then by what Otipo said. But tears were unmanly. He brushed them from his face and looked away over the heads of the crowd.

A figure caught his eye, hurrying down toward the village from the Lookout. A small figure. Jemmy Kane. A moment later Jemmy's voice was in every ear, shrilling out with all its force:

'A sail! A sail!'

Chapter 6

*T*HE cry was taken up: 'A sail! A sail!' The sighting of a sail was the most exciting event that ever took place on Halcyon. Islanders switched back instantly from the other-world of Otipo's and Mua's dance, and began running down toward the landing-place.

Luke Jonas shambled over to the Meeting-House and rang the Calling Bell loudly, again and again. The people who hadn't been watching Otipo and Mua began to emerge from their houses. Among them was the Reader, buttoning up his jacket as he came. Nobody needed to be told what the sensation was. All except the most ancient joined in the general descent to the beach.

The boat had a fair wind for its approach to the island, and came in rapidly. Its sail was high and triangular, with the short edge at the top and the long sides held to mast and spar, so that, full of wind, it looked crescent-shaped. It was a canoe with outrigger, like the one Otipo and Mua had arrived in, but a good deal bigger, with several people on board. In the stern stood a man with a steering-oar: an expert. He had seen the opening in the reef; had seen, no doubt, the waiting people. The boat ran in sweetly between the rocks; no islander could have done it better. With sail now flapping free, it ran up on to the sparkling black sand.

'It's more of *them*!' Dan Wilde exclaimed. 'What do you make of that?'

There were five men and five women in the boat. They were of similar physique and appearance to Otipo and Mua, but all fully adult; and though two or three of them seemed weak and had to be helped ashore, they were in better shape than the earlier arrivals had been. The last to land was the steersman, who was tall and muscular and stayed a little distant from the others.

The newcomers smiled, made obviously friendly gestures, and called what appeared to be greetings in a strange tongue.

By tacit consent the islanders made way for Otipo and Mua to come forward. They hailed the newcomers with astonishment and delight, and all of them began talking excitedly together in their own language. The new arrivals embraced Otipo, and in turn knelt before Mua. It was some time before their excitement allowed them to take notice of the Halcyon people, who stood around in a semi-circle, watching silently.

The Reader, slow on his feet, was the last to arrive on the beach. The ranks opened again so that he could get to the front. He surveyed the scene, then demanded sternly, 'What's all this about?'

Otipo turned to him.

'These are some of my people,' he explained. 'They live, they go to another island, but no food, no friends. So they . . .' Otipo came to a halt, unable to say what he wanted. He spoke in his own tongue to Thomas, who was standing near the front.

'They were turned away from an island near their own,' Thomas told the Reader. 'So they came on here. It's taken them a long time.'

'Many, many days,' Otipo confirmed.

'And why should *we* want them?' the Reader demanded. 'Why should they stay here, more than anywhere else?'

'They haven't asked to stay,' said Thomas, 'yet.'

After his first surprise and delight, Otipo now looked uncertain.

'They are good people,' he said. 'My people.'

The man who had steered the canoe called to Otipo and spoke rapidly and insistently to him.

'Tamaru says,' Otipo told the Reader, 'if not wanted, they ask to stay until a big ship comes which can take them to . . .'

Again he conferred with Thomas.

'To the mainland,' said Thomas.

'Could be *years* before a big ship comes to Halcyon,' the Reader said. 'And one of these days, young Thomas, I shall want to know how you come to understand this heathen lingo of theirs.'

Thomas said nothing. Another of the incomers called to Otipo.

'They hungry,' Otipo said.

'Oh, *are* they?' said the Reader sourly.

'Why don't the Bad One feed his own?' demanded Sarah Jonas, pushing forward to stand beside her brother.

'Have sense, woman!' said Uncle Abel. 'The Bad One don't have nothing to do with this!''

'How do *you* know?' said Sarah. 'Impudent old feller you are!'

Jacob Wilde stepped forward.

'They'll have to stay here tonight, Reader,' he said. 'I reckon we should put them in the Meeting-House. There's food there, left over from the Feast. And then I suppose you'll want to call another Island Meeting to decide what to do with them.'

The Reader nodded. 'I can't see nothing wrong with that,' he said. 'Take them up to the Meeting-House, the whole lot of 'em. The first two can go there as well.'

'And what about the boat?' somebody asked.

'Draw it up safe and leave it. And nobody's to touch it. There might be disease in it for all we know, or some kind of curse. So keep the children off it or you'll be in trouble.'

'There's things inside it,' Jacob Wilde remarked. 'Blankets, pots with water in, a bit of stuff that looks like dried meat. And spears. Half a dozen of them, nasty long things, sharp enough to skewer folk on.'

'You take charge of the spears, Jacob,' said the Reader. 'The other stuff can go up with them to the Meeting-House. And make sure they're locked in. Seth Attwood, you and Luke better keep guard alternately. Ring that bell if there's any trouble. We don't want to be all murdered in our beds.'

'Do they look like they'd murder anyone in their beds?' demanded Abel scornfully. 'You never saw anyone as gentle-looking. Did *my* two murder *me* in my bed?'

'You haven't even got a bed to be murdered in, Abel Oakes!' snapped Sarah.

Abel wasn't listening to her. He looked wistfully after Otipo and Mua as they were guided with the newcomers up the path toward the village, talking nonstop with their compatriots.

'My two,' he repeated wistfully to Molly. 'They don't look like mine any more, now they've got their own folk to be with. Oh well, I suppose it's only natural. But I've liked having them, while they were there. Made the cave seem like a home, which is more than it's been these fifty years.'

'They'll be back, I expect,' said Molly.

'It'll be lonely there tonight,' Abel said.

'Come and stay with us for a few days,' Hester Reeves suggested.

Abel seemed startled at first by the idea. 'I've not spent a night away from my cave since Jess died,' he said. But after some thought he remarked, 'Oh well, there's no avoiding change. And it'll be a good thing for me to be here in the village and see what's going on.'

The newcomers were taken to the Meeting-House, where the women who had been putting away the leftover food now brought it out again and offered it. Islanders gathered round in the doorway to see what happened. The food was inspected doubtfully, to the irritation of some of the older folk, who had a respect for food based on long experience of scarcity.

'Sniffing at good eatables!' said old Aunt Annie Jonas disapprovingly.

But Otipo and Mua could be seen to be recommending it, and soon all the incomers were eating the potatoes and the little remaining meat. One or two of them pulled faces, to Aunt Annie's displeasure. They ignored the knives and forks which had been placed before them, and ate delicately with their fingers, which particularly offended Sarah.

'You can tell they ain't civilized!' she declared. 'Savages, that's what they are. And aren't hardly dressed decent, either!'

As it grew dusk, the seal-oil lamps were lit in the Meeting-House. Islanders still stood in the doorway, and Otipo made efforts at introduction between them and his own people. But both sides were overwhelmed by the strangeness of the occasion, and little contact was made. After a while Jacob Wilde came round, clearing people away from the Meeting-House and sending them off to their homes.

'Reader's orders!' he told them.

'When will the meeting be held to decide what happens?' Adam Goodall asked.

'Not till Prayer Day. We lost one good fishing day today, with it being a holiday. Can't afford to lose no more working days. We'll be out in the boats tomorrow if it stays fine.'

But it didn't. During the night the wind got up. Molly, sleeping beside Beth, was awakened by it. It howled fiercely around the houses, rising at times to a threatening crescendo. The crash of sea on rock could be heard in relentless pounding rhythm. Molly was thankful that the newcomers had landed, for they couldn't have survived in this; their frail craft would have been swamped in no time, or driven headlong on to rocks or reef.

She lay awake for a long time, listening to the wind and thinking of Otipo and Mua and the new arrivals. For a while the storm faded from her mind, and the dance of Otipo and Mua, overshadowed by the events which had followed it, came back to her in all its power: the wild and breathtaking beauty of young, swiftly-moving, almost-naked bodies. It was sinful, surely, to expose so much of yourself to the public view, contrary to the modesty on which the Teaching insisted. But it didn't *feel* sinful; on the contrary, it gave her a sense of marvellous liberation. It was unforgettable; maybe it was the greatest experience she'd ever had.

But what would happen now to Mua and Otipo and the others? She knew what the Reader thought; and there would be many islanders who would agree with him. And this wind . . .

By morning it was blowing a full Halcyon gale. No one went out, for you couldn't stand up in it. In years gone by, people had been blown fifty yards and swept to death over the cliff. Water filled the air; but it wasn't rain, it was spray. The temperature fell sharply. Fires were lit and banked up; women knitted and men did the domestic jobs they'd been neglecting; time dragged and tempers grew frayed. The Calling Bell tolled mournfully, but everyone knew it wasn't Luke who was ringing it, it was the wind.

The day wore on, and instead of blowing itself out the storm grew still more ferocious. Grousing gave way to alarm. This wind would cause damage. Not so much to houses; some thatch might be lost and some outbuildings collapse, but the village was built to stand up to storm, and stand it would. Not to stock: the sheep were hardy enough, though a few of the weaker ones might come to grief. Not to trees: apart from a few stunted fruit trees in the Dell and other sheltered spots, and the scrubby island oak which grew in the wilder parts of Halcyon and was brought home for fuel, the island was treeless. What was at risk was the crop: the staple crop.

All through a second night the storm roared away. And then toward dawn it stopped, so suddenly it might have been turned off by some superhuman hand. The sun came up into a silky blue sky, the wind was no more than a gentle breath, and it was summer again.

But cheerfulness did not return with the good weather. The Reader led another procession up to the vegetable plots: a muttering, dispirited one this time. Everyone knew what would be found. On Lifting Day there had been forty acres of flourishing potato plants. Two nights and a day of biting midsummer gale had withered the lot. The main crop would fail. Next winter animals would have to be killed to keep the islanders alive; and they would still go hungry.

'We know what brought *that* on us!' the Reader declared bitterly.

'It would have happened anyway,' said Adam Goodall.

But there were angry and jeering noises from those around.

'It's them savages!' Harry Kane proclaimed. 'We should never have let them land!'

'What, you mean we should have had a pitched battle with them on the shore?' said Adam. 'Don't be so stupid!'

'Don't you call my pal stupid, Adam Goodall!' growled Bob Attwood, clenching a fist.

'Well, it *is* stupid, to suppose that people landing here could affect the weather. Have a bit of sense!'

'Now, listen,' Harry Kane said in a reasonable tone. 'I been getting the Teaching thrown at me all my life, especially as a descendant of the Deliverer. Well, this time it's me that's reminding all of you. The Teaching says that incomers is to be rejected. But we've let this lot land, and given 'em food and somewhere to sleep. And now we're seeing the result. The very night they arrive, *this* happens, out of a clear sky! It's absolute proof. Proof positive!'

'It's nothing of the sort!' Adam said.

'Teaching or no Teaching,' remarked Alec Campbell, 'there's twelve of these people now, and a hungry winter to come. We cannot *afford* to feed them!'

There were murmurs of agreement.

'C'mon, fellers!' urged Bob. 'Let's deal with 'em now! Sooner the better!'

'Don't be in such a hurry!' the Reader told him. He turned and spoke to the gathering at large.

'There'll be no taking the law into your own hands!' he declared. 'Whether they're the Bad One's brood or not, you just leave that lot alone in the Meeting-House. There'll be a public meeting on Prayer Day, and this time it'll be the right decision, you mark my words. And *then* we'll put them back to sea in their own boat.'

'We won't, you know!' piped up Jemmy Kane, who had just run along the track to join the group.

'You keep your mouth shut, young Jemmy Kane!' the Reader said. 'This ain't a matter for children. If the meeting decides so, we'll do it, of course.'

'We won't!' repeated Jemmy. 'Because we can't!' He spoke

gleefully, enjoying the news he'd brought. 'Because they ain't got a boat no more. A high tide come in and swep' it out to sea. And then bashed it against the rocks and smashed it to bits. Nobody'll repair that. Not Uncle Abel, not the Bad One himself, *nobody*! That boat's finished!'

The Reader was nonplussed, but only for a moment.

'We'll see,' he said. 'If you're right, young Jemmy, well then, we'll have to dump 'em on Kingfisher, that's all. The result'll be the same. There's no way they'll get off Kingfisher without a boat. And, talking of boats, we can't have both of ours lying idle. Jacob, you better keep your crew ashore today for safety's sake, 'cause if the savages did break loose there'd only be women, children and old men to deal with them. But as for you, Harry, the sooner you take *Seamew* out the better.'

'Oh, sure,' said Harry. 'Come on, fellers. I expect the savages could do with a nice bit of fish for their tea!'

In the village, the day was an ordinary one, but shot through with subdued excitement. Women washed clothes in the brook, then gossiped together in each other's houses, speculating about the incomers and the prospects for the coming winter. Children minded the animals, fetched and carried as required, and apart from that hung around aimlessly, for Halcyon children had never learned to play. The men of Jacob's crew also stayed around the village, ready to carry out their defensive duties if necessary. The Reader had acted diplomatically in sending Harry Kane's boat to sea, for his crew contained most of the malcontents.

The New People were still confined to the Meeting-House. Luke Jonas guarded the door, wielding a big stick, and wouldn't let Molly and Thomas inside. Luke was enjoying the present drama; he had never felt so important in his life. Eventually Molly and Thomas managed to peer in through a back window. Most of the incomers were huddled disconsolately together, aware by now that they were prisoners; only the tall helmsman stood proudly aloof. Thomas attracted Otipo's attention, but before they could talk to any purpose Luke came bustling round to the back of the Meeting-House with his big stick and drove Molly and Thomas away.

In mid-afternoon Harry Kane's boat came in. In spite of good conditions it had caught nothing. The men stomped up to the village, bad-tempered and glowering, and were met by Jacob's crew, to whom they complained loudly.

Dick Reeves was among those who talked to them.

'You got to admit,' he told his family afterwards, 'these folk brought bad luck if nothing more.'

'That's against common sense,' said Hester stoutly.

'Maybe,' her husband said. 'But there's plenty of things in life we don't understand. All we got to go on's the Teaching.' And even those islanders who prided themselves most on being steady and reasonable seemed to share a feeling that the Meeting-House, with the dozen strange people in it, radiated some kind of threat to their tranquillity and wellbeing.

'I feel it myself,' Adam Goodall admitted. In fact the only people totally unaffected by any such feeling were Thomas, who cared little for the Teaching and much for Mua and Otipo, and Uncle Abel, whose eccentricity stopped at nothing.

'Lot o' nonsense!' he declared. 'I seen too many crop failures already in my life, and they happens any time. And this warn't the first summer storm we've had, and won't be the last. As for the Teaching, I don't know that I take William Jonas's word for that.'

'He didn't make it up, you know,' said Dick. 'It was handed down to him.'

'I dare say. But I remember my grandpa telling me that if the truth was known the Book might not say what it's supposed to say. And he got that from *his* grandpa, who was one of the first folk born on the island.'

'I've heard that from you before, more than once, Abel Oakes,' said Dick, 'and I don't believe it no more now than I ever did.'

'There, there, Dick, you leave Uncle Abel alone,' said Hester soothingly.

'Then he can leave the Teaching alone,' said Dick. And the old man was silent.

Toward evening, two of the women, acting on the Reader's instructions, took more food to the incomers: potatoes, fish and milk. They were watched sullenly by a ring of islanders. All of them had known food shortage often enough and expected to know it again.

A little later, half a dozen of the younger island men, led by Harry Kane and Bob Attwood, converged on the Meeting-House.

'You can't go in!' squeaked Luke.

'We want to see what they're up to!' said Harry Kane.

'They're not up to anything. They're just sitting there.'

'Get out of the way, Luke Jonas!' Bob Attwood said. 'Remember what happens when you don't do what me and Harry say?'

Luke had been bullied by Harry and Bob as a boy, and was afraid of them. But the Reader's authority counted with him even more.

'I tell you, you can't go in! Reader's orders! You heard! Reader's orders!'

Harry and Bob shoved past him and stood in the doorway of the Meeting-House, gazing at the people inside.

'Sitting on the floor!' said Bob. 'Like blooming heathens! Folk what knows how to behave sits on boxes!'

'Here! What you got behind your backs?' demanded Luke. 'You got sticks and stones! You just take 'em away again!' He bawled at the top of his voice, 'Adam! Adam!'

Adam had seen the little knot of men moving toward the Meeting-House. He came running up, with Dick Reeves and Thomas. Meanwhile, Abby Jonas sped away toward the Reader's house.

Bob had his hands around Luke's throat.

'They got to keep out, Adam, ain't they?' Luke gasped. And, once again, 'Reader's orders!'

In a moment there was a scrimmage in progress. Sticks and

stones were dropped and fists used. Adam dragged Bob away from Luke. Jacob and Dan Wilde arrived, and Jacob, who had long seen Harry Kane as a threat to authority, pitched into him. The New People came crowding to the Meeting-House door and watched in amazement.

The battle didn't last long. Halcyon had no tradition of violence or of disregard for the Reader's instructions. Two or three blows were enough to cool men's anger and turn it to shock at what they were doing. Only Bob Attwood and Adam Goodall, who detested each other, were determined to make a fight of it, and soon the others were standing back while they slogged it out. Bob, the heavier man, had just sent Adam staggering with a blow to the side of the head when Luke yelled,

'The Reader! Reader's coming!'

The Reader approached with dignity. Everyone fell back. Jacob Wilde tried to look like one who had been restoring order. Adam and Bob stopped fighting but continued to glower at each other. Harry mopped a bleeding nose. The New People disappeared from the Meeting-House doorway, and Luke slammed the door and put his back to it.

'So *that*'s what we've come to!' the Reader said, outraged. 'I'd have thought better of *you*, Adam Goodall!'

Adam, breathing hard, said nothing, but Luke spoke up:

'Harry and Bob was trying to get at the savages!'

'Oh, *was* they?' said the Reader. He turned to the villagers who by now had crowded around. 'You see? You who was in doubt, just take note of that! Less than three days we've had the savages here, and look what's happened! The worst storm ever known, houses damaged, the tater crop ruined, and now *fighting*! Fighting on Halcyon! If that ain't the work of evil, I don't know what is!'

'And no fish in the nets!' shouted one of the men from behind.

'And no fish in the nets!' echoed the Reader. 'That's five bad things in three days! Strife and starvation, that's what they're bringing us to! Well, all I can say is, I'll expect every grown person to be at the meeting on Prayer Day, and I'll be expecting you to put right the mistake you made last time. And Deliverer help us all!'

Early on Prayer Day, the incomers were marched to Jacob Wilde's cottage, so that the public meeting could be held in the Meeting-House. Molly and Thomas, having no evidence to give this time, were not allowed in, but watched and waited outside.

It was a fine morning, but they were not hopeful. 'It's a foregone conclusion, I'm afraid,' Adam had told them.

Nothing could be heard of the proceedings from outside, except an occasional raised voice, usually that of Abel Oakes. But Molly and Thomas didn't have long to wait. The meeting was much shorter than the previous one had been. Quite soon the Meeting-House door opened and, in accordance with custom, the Reader led the way out.

He wasn't walking with his usual lone dignity. Uncle Abel scurried alongside, trying to clutch his shoulder with a bony hand while haranguing him. Jacob Wilde and Luke Jonas held the old man off with some difficulty.

'Disgraceful, Will Jonas!' Abel was shouting. 'Disgraceful! Wicked! It'll be the end of them! They'll starve! It's as bad as killing them!'

'The Bad One should have thought of that before he sent them here!' said the Reader. 'We seen through his wiles this time!'

Adam tried to draw Abel gently away, but was shaken off. He gave up the attempt and came over to Molly and Thomas, his face set and unsmiling.

'I don't have to tell you what happened,' he said. 'It was just as I thought. They're to be taken to Kingfisher, right away, and left there for as long as they live. Which I'm afraid may not be long.'

Chapter 7

*T*HE decision was carried out at once. There wasn't any time to spare if the island boats were to get to Kingfisher and back within the day.

The Reader was taking no chances. The half-dozen ancient muskets which made up the island's armoury had been brought out and cleaned the night before, and were shared among the two boat-crews. Other islanders who escorted the New People down to the landing-place carried stout clubs. The unarmed incomers could hardly have offered resistance, and didn't try. They moved with quiet dignity, as if resigned to their fate, and did not speak, even to each other.

Six of the New People were allotted to each of the longboats, *Shearwater* and *Seamew*, and each boat had a diminished crew of four. As usual, Jacob Wilde helmed *Shearwater* and Harry Kane *Seamew*. Adam, at his own request, was left out of Jacob's crew on this occasion, and remained ashore. Abel Oakes, shouting abuse, pursued the boats down the inlet and bawled after them as they pulled out to sea.

'If it was anyone but you, Abel,' remarked the Reader, 'I'd have him put in the stocks for that. But seeing it's you, and we all know there's no fool like an old fool, we shall treat you with the contempt you deserve.'

'Contempt? What do you think I feel for *you?*' Abel retorted; and then he broke down and wept. 'Those are *my* two. The only children I ever had, and you send them to die! Nobody can live on Kingfisher!'

'Come now, Uncle,' said Hester Reeves, putting her arm through the old man's. 'Come home with me. Let me give you a warm drink. Maybe they'll manage on Kingfisher. There's water there, I'm told, and seabirds nest on the cliffs like they do here.'

'I been to Kingfisher,' said Abel, 'which is more than any of you ever have. I know what's on Kingfisher. Them cliffs ain't climbable. There's just a bit of flatland by the beach, and you can't get off it without you have a boat. I seen the bones of castaways there. They died of starvation, and there wasn't nobody to bury them.'

Reluctantly the old man accepted Hester's arm and shambled off to the Reeveses' cottage, with none of the spring in his step that had been there a few days earlier.

Later Molly and Thomas walked up to the Lookout, to watch the two boats making their way to Kingfisher. They had sails up now, and were tacking against the wind, moving in step with each other and going about in unison.

'They'll be back by nightfall if it stays fine,' Thomas said. 'Without Otipo or Mua or any of them.' And then, in distress, 'How could people let it happen? It's not right, Moll, it isn't. They can't believe the Deliverer wants *that*!'

'I don't know,' Molly said. 'I don't know what the Deliverer wants. I don't know anything.'

'Nobody knows anything on Halcyon,' said Thomas. 'Sometimes I wish I was away from here. In the Outside World.'

Molly was startled. She didn't really believe that anything existed outside Halcyon. And she had feelings for the island that she could never have put into words. She loved Halcyon: the ever-changing patterns of sea and sky, the wind moving over the grassy upland, the black dramatic cliffs and glittering black sand below, the Peak soaring above. Like the stormy petrels she was happy in wind and rain; like the island's few wild flowers she opened when the sun shone.

'But the Outside World is all wickedness, isn't it?' she asked.

'It can't be wickeder than what's happening now. Abel's right. I don't understand how people can do such things to other people.'

'Well, the meeting decided,' Molly said uneasily.

'Yes, but there's some things folk haven't any right to decide.'

'Adam thinks like we do,' Molly said. 'And so does Beth. And I reckon our mum does, too.'

'And all of them either young or women,' Thomas said. 'What's the good of being young on Halcyon?'

'Or a woman,' said Molly.

'We're all cooped up together here, and when we get these beliefs about folk bringing bad luck or casting the evil eye or the Bad One being behind something, they kind of stick around and we can't get rid of them. Though as for the New People, Adam reckons it was Alec Campbell that came out with the truth of the matter. What folk really have in their minds, he says, if they did but know it, is that we'll find it hard enough to feed ourselves. There's a hungry winter coming.'

'I couldn't go far from Halcyon, you know,' Molly said, only half listening. 'Whatever happened, I couldn't.'

Toward evening, thirty or more islanders made their way to the Lookout, to watch for the return of the boats. The sea was still calm, but the voyage between Halcyon and Kingfisher was long enough for it to change completely. What began as an easy trip could end as a perilous one.

There was some alarm when only one boat could be seen, far off, crawling homeward across the wide expanse of water. No one could tell at first which boat it was. Adam ran down to the village to borrow the Reader's telescope, but even with its aid it was some time before any distinguishing feature could be recognised. And still the second boat did not appear.

'It's Jacob,' Adam said to Thomas at last. 'And Dan, and your dad, and Wilf Jonas. The first crew. What's happened to the second one?'

No one could answer. By the time the boat had rounded the tip of the island and approached the landing-place, the Reader himself was there to meet it.

'Where's Harry's boat?' he demanded at once.

Jacob Wilde looked uneasy as he stepped ashore.

'Coming back tomorrow,' he said.

'Coming tomorrow? What happened?'

'Nothing happened. They thought, seeing they were there, they'd go round to the other side of Kingfisher. There's said to be wild goats at the rocky end. They reckoned they might shoot one or two.'

'Shoot goats?' The Reader was outraged. 'Who said they could go shooting goats?'

'Nobody said they could do that.'

'They know we don't land on Kingfisher, none of us. That's Sin Island, that is. Strictly forbidden, in the Teaching.'

'I know, Reader,' said Jacob. 'But I suppose Harry thought, seeing we'd come to Kingfisher anyway, there was no harm in going a bit further.'

'No harm in going a bit further!' The Reader could hardly get the words out for anger. Calming himself with an effort, he asked, 'What about the savages?'

'Oh, they weren't any trouble. We put 'em ashore at this end, on the flatland. They didn't try to resist; they couldn't. We had them covered with the muskets.'

'And why didn't you make Harry come straight back, like he was told?'

'Listen, William,' said Jacob, who was beginning to sound irritated himself. 'You wasn't there, right? Now, tell me what I could have done when Harry shouted across that they was going round the other side. Seems to me nobody could have stopped them. It's when they get guns in their hands, that's what turns their heads. With powder so scarce, it's not often they get a chance to shoot anything.'

'I might have known!' The Reader groaned. Then, bitterly, 'This island's getting out of hand. Folk doing just what they feel like doing, regardless of whether it's sinful, regardless of the Teaching. Don't it count for nothing no more, what the Reader says? Just wait till Harry Kane gets back here! I'll give him a piece of my mind!'

'Let's hope the weather stays good,' said Jacob. 'If it turned bad, they might have to stay on Kingfisher for a week or more.'

'It's all part of the same thing!' declared Sarah Jonas. 'The hand of the Bad One has fallen on Halcyon. I don't know what we done to deserve it. I'm sure, whatever it is, it ain't the Reader and me that's responsible. *We* ain't disobeyed the Teaching. But I wouldn't be surprised if Harry and that lot was to bring back sin from Kingfisher. As for the savages, we brought this on ourselves by being kind to them. It's no good being kind-hearted when you're dealing with the Bad One. Why couldn't they have just been taken out to sea and dropped overboard?'

'The Teaching says . . .' began the Reader patiently.

'Aye, so we're told. I wish I knew what it *did,* say. Things get changed when they're handed down by word of mouth.'

'That'll do, Sarah Jonas!' the Reader told her sharply. 'Sounds to me as if *you're* questioning authority now.' And then, 'I wish this hadn't happened. There's been boats lost around Kingfisher or on the way there before. We can't afford to lose another boat and crew!'

'Harry's a good helmsman,' said Jacob. 'They'll be back tomorrow, don't worry.'

'I should hope so. But he'll be in trouble, I can tell you. This island can't get along if folk just please themselves and do whatever they take it into their heads to do!'

Old Annie Jonas, who didn't think of anything much these days except her stomach, said, 'They might bring back some goat meat, though.' She licked her lips. 'I like a nice bit of goat flesh.'

'Shame on you, Aunt Annie!' said the Reader. 'Beware the sin of gluttony, especially an old woman like you that doesn't need to eat much. Well, Harry and his crew better be back tomorrow and ready to answer for themselves, that's all I can say!' He turned on his heel and headed back to the village.

But *Seamew* didn't come back the next day, or the day after. On the third and fourth days, Halcyon was shrouded in fog, and no islander in his senses would have dreamed of trying to cross from Kingfisher; but it occurred to many people that Harry might have set out before the fog came down, and with the ocean so large and the island so small it wouldn't be difficult to lose your way and never find it again.

The loss of four able-bodied men, a boat, and half the guns and ammunition would be a disaster. Even the thought of it was enough to fill most minds and prevent people from brooding on the fate of the New People, which otherwise might have troubled some consciences. On the fifth day, when the skies were clear and the sea calm, the Reader struggled several times to the Lookout with his telescope, scanning the horizons all round for any sign of the boat. But there was none.

On one of these occasions, Jacob Wilde went with him, and the two of them, Reader and Senior Elder, quarrelled openly in front of a group of islanders. No such thing had happened on Halcyon in living memory. The Teaching ordained that all must live peaceably together and that neither hand nor voice must be raised in anger. Lesser islanders hadn't always managed to observe this rule, and heated moments weren't unknown. But for the Reader and the Senior Elder to quarrel in public was deeply shocking.

The Reader upbraided Jacob yet again for allowing Harry's desertion to happen.

'What it boils down to, Jacob,' he said, 'is that you ain't got no natural power of leadership. You was in charge of the party, and Harry knew it. You should have made it clear that you wasn't standing no nonsense. If *I'd* been in your position, and in the prime of life like you are, this wouldn't have happened.'

'That's what *you* say!' Jacob retorted. 'Talking's easy. The fact is, you wasn't there, and if you had been I don't see what you could have done that I didn't!'

'A sign from me,' said the Reader, 'and Harry Kane'd have

come to heel. He'd have recognized a natural superior. Seems to me, Jacob, that you're not the man to be Reader after me. Time I was looking for another successor.'

'Maybe,' said Jacob. 'I ain't that keen to have the job anyway. But I'll tell you this, William. If I'd been Reader on this occasion, I'd not have let Harry choose the crew he did. Him and Bob Attwood and Alec Campbell and Len Wilde! They're the four biggest ne'erdowells on the island. Len's as bad as the rest, even if he *is* my cousin.' He paused, then went on after a moment's thought, 'Listen, we'll take *you* across to Kingfisher and find them, and then you can show us how you bring them to heel!'

But the Reader didn't want Jacob's boat to leave Halcyon, whether he himself was on board or not.

'*Shearwater*'s the only seaworthy boat we have at the moment,' he said. 'If that was lost, what'd happen to us? Everyone on Halcyon'd starve. Or suppose a ship was to come at last while we was away? There wouldn't be a boat to send out to it.'

'And there's another thing,' said Adam Goodall. 'Harry and Bob and the others are armed. They've got muskets, and powder and shot. What if they were to resist?'

'I can't believe they'd fire on us,' the Reader said, though he didn't sound too sure. And then, as another thought struck him, 'Of course, there's the savages, too. Harry's lot might have had a fight with the savages. They might even have been *et*!'

'The savages haven't any weapons,' Jacob pointed out. 'They couldn't fight men with guns.'

'Aye, but savages is cunning and treacherous,' said the Reader. 'And with the Bad One backing them, too, I don't like to think what might happen.'

'If you ask me,' said Jacob, 'the most likely thing is that Harry's crew are still round the other side, shooting. And they'll come back soon, because there's nothing on Kingfisher to stay for. We just got to be patient for another day or two.'

'I suppose so,' the Reader said. He sighed. 'To think that

only on Lifting Day things were looking so good, and now we have all these problems . . . There's no end to the wiles of the Bad One. Oh well, it's Prayer Day again in a couple of days' time. I'll make up some special prayers to the Deliverer to sort things out for us. Let's hope that does the trick.'

Molly had gone into storms of weeping. Beth and Thomas and their mother were at a loss. They had always thought of Thomas as the sensitive one and of Molly as strong, calm, sensible, solid. The change was as baffling to Molly herself as to anyone else. They could all understand and share her grief and anger over the fate of Otipo and Mua and their people; but when she was torn with sudden great sobs of physical origin which might overwhelm her at any time of the day or night, it seemed to Molly as if her body was outside herself and suffering torments she only half knew about.

Beth, who slept with Molly and shared with her a succession of restless nights, found her sister alternately a close intimate and a stranger. Sometimes Molly would clasp her fiercely, other times she would turn violently away, and again and again would come the rending sobs. On the morning before Prayer Day, after a particularly disturbed night, Molly slept on long after daybreak, and Beth left her in the sleeping-place.

'I think she's in love with the incomer lad,' Beth remarked sagely to her mother and Thomas.

'I reckon you're right,' Hester agreed. 'You're putting into words what I've thought for a long time. But she doesn't know it herself. She's always known she's intended for Dan Wilde. There never was any future in Otipo. It's a hard thing to say, but the sooner she forgets him the better.'

'*Forget* him?' echoed Thomas. He was furious with his mother. 'How do you expect anyone to forget? I'm not going to forget, as long as I live. I don't know how you can say such a thing, when they're probably dying slowly from day to day, all of them.'

'You know who'll be hit hardest of all?' Hester Reeves asked.

Thomas nodded.

'Yes. Uncle Abel.'

'I haven't seen him since the day it happened,' Hester said. 'I brought him back here from the landing-place, but he wouldn't stay. Said he wanted to get back to the cave and tell his Jess about it.'

'Poor old feller!' said Beth. 'He needs some human company. There's no comfort in somebody that's been dead sixty years.'

'I'm not sure about that last bit,' said Hester. 'Uncle Abel's gone on living with her ever since, in his own way, and it does comfort him. But yes, he needs real company as well. Why don't you three go and see him today? Now the New People have gone, the Reader won't mind. You can take Abel one of my cranberry puddings and some of Daisy's milk. He was always partial to Daisy's milk.'

Molly, haggard and unusually silent, merely nodded when Beth woke her and proposed this expedition. On the way across to Abel's cave she said nothing, and the words spoken by Beth and Thomas seemed to patter meaninglessly on the outside of her mind, making no impression. Passing the ruin of Jonathan Wilde's cottage, which usually sent a shiver down her spine, she felt nothing; it was just a heap of old stones. She crossed the three steep gulches so carelessly that she might well have fallen and slid perilously in a little avalanche of stone and dirt to the bottom of any of them; but sure feet and casual expertise saw her through.

They turned down Billygoat, the last of the gulches, and walked from its mouth across the sand toward the skull-shaped cave. Empty now of Otipo and Mua, it seemed to Molly as devoid of life as if it really were a skull. Of Abel himself, as they approached, there was no sign.

'A-bell! Uncle A-bell!' Thomas called.

'Uncle A-bell!' Beth took up the cry. But there was no response.

Otipo's and Mua's boat had been drawn up into the mouth

of the cave, where it was well above the high water mark and had been sheltered from the gale. It seemed to be undamaged.

'Uncle A-bell!' Thomas called again. Still no response. Alarmed, they walked past the boat and through the outer compartment to the inner cave. The old man was there, lying on the ledge that served him for a bed and covered with his usual heap of sheepskins. He opened his eyes as they approached, and closed them again.

At the sight of him, Molly came back to life. She was in the world again, not detached from it. Anxiety flooded through her.

'Are you all right, Uncle?' she demanded.

'I'm all right. Go away.'

'You're not sick or anything?'

'Sick at heart, that's all. I suppose that ain't anything. I'm not ill.'

'I know how you feel,' Molly said. 'But you got to take care of yourself. Have you had anything to eat today?'

'I don't want anything. I told you, go away.'

'We're not going away,' Thomas said. 'Look, we brought you some of Daisy's milk, and a cranberry pudding. Are you well enough to get up and eat it? It's chilly in here, isn't it? Let's make a fire.'

'I don't want no food,' the old man said. 'And I don't want no fire, neither. All I want is to be left in peace. It won't be for long.'

'What do you mean by that?' asked Beth.

'I mean,' said Abel, 'that I've had my time in this world, as much of it as I can do with. I don't want to go on living no more.'

Once again Molly knew how the old man felt. But instead of sympathising she heard herself saying crossly, 'Oh, come on, don't be so silly!' And it was the right thing to say. In spite of his words, Abel seemed stimulated. He sat up, and there was more vigour in his voice.

'You know how old I am?' he asked them.

All three shook their heads.

'Nor do I, exactly,' Abel admitted. 'But my dad said I was born the year of the *Jonquil* wreck. That'd make me over eighty. Eighty-three, maybe, or eighty-five. It don't make much difference which. I've had enough. They took my children away from me, and I don't want to stay here thinking about them dying.'

'You've never thought you might be able to do something about it?' Thomas asked.

'What can I do? William Jonas won't change his mind, I can tell you that. Obstinate old fool that he is!'

The last words were spoken energetically. Abel took a cup of goat's milk from Thomas's hand and swallowed it, apparently without thinking.

'Adam says we got to keep on trying to persuade folk,' said Beth. 'He reckons they might still regret what they done, when they think of the New People actually dying over there. And if there was enough who felt like that, he says, they could get the Reader to call another meeting.'

'*That* won't work!' Thomas declared. 'Right now, they're worrying about Harry Kane and *Seamew*, not about the New People.' He frowned. 'Still, there must be *something* we can do.'

'Maybe we could get over to Kingfisher ourselves!' said Molly.

There was a startled silence. Then,

'Why not?' asked Thomas. 'I've wanted to do that all my life!'

'Well,' said Abel. 'Let's forget that it's forbidden. Let's forget the trouble you'd be in when the Reader found out. Just remember you need a longboat to cross to Kingfisher. At the moment there's only *Shearwater*. Nobody's going to let you have her. And if you *could* get hold of her, you'd need strong, skilled, grown men to manage her. You two youngsters couldn't do it.'

There was another, chastened, silence. Then a further thought struck Molly.

'What about the boat Otipo and Mua came in?' she asked. 'The canoe?'

Thomas's eyes lit up.

'Could we?' he asked. 'Would she make it?'

Abel looked dubious.

'I don't know as I want you to set out for Kingfisher in a boat as light as that,' he said. 'Fifteen miles to cover, and I don't need to tell you about the gusts and eddies, and the current round South Point. You'd be over in no time, or else swept miles away.'

'Seeing it brought Otipo and Mua a thousand miles,' said Thomas, 'I reckon it'll take us to Kingfisher. And I can sail it. I practised with them, you know.'

'It was a miracle that brought them to me,' Abel said. His eyes filled with tears.

'Perhaps we could bring them back,' Molly suggested.

'Don't be daft, Moll,' said Thomas. 'They couldn't be hidden for long. They'd soon be found.'

'What would you do if you *did* get over there?' Abel asked; then, 'Here, give me a bit of that pudding, Thomas. I might eat something after all.'

'We could get some food together and take it,' said Molly.

'You couldn't take enough to feed a dozen people for any length of time,' Abel pointed out. He was getting interested, all the same.

'What they need is to be able to get their own food,' he said. 'This time of year, there's crayfish inshore. I got spare nets and lines they could have.'

'What about some potatoes to plant?' Thomas asked. 'And some vegetable seed? And if we could get a few chickens to take across . . .'

'Now, now, young Thomas, you're letting your imagination run away with you. There ain't no soil on Kingfisher fit to grow taters or anything else. There's just a strip of sandy flatland at this side, and the rest's all rock. It's not a place folk could live on for long.'

'Still,' said Thomas, 'While there's life there's hope.'

'They'd need something to keep them warm, mind you,' Abel mused. 'It gets cold, nights, even at this time of year, and I reckon they're not used to it. Still, I got plenty of sheepskins I could give them, and maybe some old clothes. There's some that was Jess's, all those years ago.'

Then his face clouded.

'I'm talking daft,' he said. 'It can't be done. You'd be drowning yourselves, most like, and what good would that do?'

'I'd risk it,' said Molly. The deadening weight of grief, already shifted by her concern for Abel, rolled aside at the thought of doing something practical about seeing the incomers again. 'I'd risk it,' she repeated.

'If we picked our time right, it mightn't be such a risk,' said Thomas. 'It's calm today. Might stay calm for a few days now. It often does at this time of year.'

'And it might blow up to a gale within the hour,' said Abel, 'like it did last week. One thing I learned in all my years is, never trust Halcyon weather.'

There was silence for a few moments. Then Abel went on,

'Of course, I could come with you. I know all the reefs and currents, and the places where the gusts hit you. You'd be safer with me on board than by yourselves.'

'You couldn't, Uncle,' said Thomas. 'Not at your age.'

'Course I could!' declared Abel. 'I'm very fit, let me tell you, for a man of . . . how old did I say I am? Eighty-five? I dare say I got it wrong. Seventy-five'd be more like it.'

'You were ready to die a little while ago,' Thomas reminded him.

'Aye, well, I recover quick,' said Abel. 'Always did. I'm strong, you know. I'm a better man than William Jonas.' He paused. 'All the same,' he added thoughtfully, 'you got to treat the sea with respect. And then, if you get to Kingfisher, you might have trouble with Harry Kane and his riff-raff. You'd do well to have a younger able-bodied man than what I am, to back me up. I'm in pretty good shape for a man of seventy, but there's a limit to what I can do with only a lad and lass like you to help.'

'Another able-bodied man?' said Thomas. 'It mightn't be easy to find one.'

'Maybe if you was to go tomorrow,' said Beth, 'my Adam

would go with you, that being Prayer Day and no fishing to do.'

'Now that's a grand idea!' said Abel. 'Adam Goodall's a fine lad. I've known him all his life, and his dad and grandad before him.'

The old man was getting enthusiastic.

'Here, Molly!' he said. 'You'll find a bit of stew in that pan over there. Let's make ourselves a fire — there in the corner, where the vent takes the smoke away — and heat it up and get warm. And let's make a proper plan. It won't be so risky if you have Adam Goodall and Abel Oakes with you. They think I'm an old fool, but I forgotten more about the sea around here than they ever knew. I'll get you to Kingfisher, and get you back, too!'

'I could eat some stew,' said a voice from the entrance to the cave.

'Who's that? Who is it?' Abel was instantly on the alert, his voice full of suspicion.

'It's only me.' Jemmy Kane stepped forward, unconcerned. 'You didn't know you had *me* with you, did you?'

'Little perisher!' snorted Abel. 'You get away home, or I'll . . .'

'How did you come to be here, Jemmy?' Thomas asked.

'I follered you across. You and Beth and Molly.'

'Why?'

'I wondered what you was up to, that's all. I like knowing what people's up to.'

'You should be at home, minding your own business, not follering folks around,' said Abel severely.

'Should be at home?' echoed Jemmy. 'Don't make me laugh! Call it a home, when my dad's away? It's not much of a home when he's there, but now he ain't there it ain't no home at all!'

'Aren't you supposed to be staying with your Aunt Lucy Attwood?' Thomas inquired.

'She don't want me,' Jemmy said. 'Nor I don't want her, neither.'

'Aye, well, I'm not surprised he don't want to stay with

Lazy Lucy,' said Abel, looking on Jemmy with more sympathy. 'She never did keep a clean house. But you got no business snooping around, young Jemmy. You're too inquisitive by half!'

'I heard you talking,' said Jemmy. 'You're thinking of going to Kingfisher, ain't you? Well, if you go, I'm coming too!'

'Oh no, you're not!' said Thomas.

'Oh yes, I am!' retorted Jemmy. 'I want to go and look for my dad!'

'We're not going in search of Harry Kane,' said Thomas.

'Though we might find him,' said Molly thoughtfully, 'whether we're looking for him or not.'

'I got a *right* to come!' Jemmy insisted. 'My dad's all the family I have. I wouldn't be no trouble, I'd be useful. I'm quick in a boat, you know.'

'It's only a light canoe,' Thomas said. 'If we took you, there'd be less room for things the New People need.'

'I wouldn't take up much room. And I don't weigh much. If you want to save space or weight, you should leave Molly!'

Molly was furious.

'*Oh*, no!' she said grimly. 'It was my idea. If anyone gets left, it won't be me!'

'Now listen, young Jemmy Kane,' said Abel. 'If *I* get drowned, it don't matter. I'm an old man, sixty-five years old. If Molly and Thomas was to get drowned, it'd matter, seeing they got their lives in front of them, but they're old enough to know what they're doing, and I won't stop them. But as for you, I'm not going to let you risk it, and that's definite. You ever thought, Jemmy, what drowning'd be like? Or being attacked by a shark, which these seas is full of?'

'You know something, Uncle Abel?' Jemmy said. 'When we was here before, I went into the back of this cave. I move quick and light, you know. And I seen . . .'

He paused for effect.

'You seen what?' The sharp, alarmed note was back in Abel's voice.

'I seen that iron chest you got there.'

'Why, you young . . .'

'And seeing I like to know things, I keep wondering what's in it.'

'You won't get into that, I can tell you!'

'Maybe not. It's got a good lock on it.'

'So you tried, eh?'

'There's some on the island that could force it,' said Jemmy calmly. 'But if you was to let me come to Kingfisher, I might forget I'd ever seen it, mightn't I?'

Thomas, Beth and Molly stared. This was the first they'd heard of any iron chest. Abel was clearly shaken, but took a grip on himself.

'Jemmy Kane,' he said in a strained voice, 'you're enough to make a man believe in the Bad One. You and your dad! If the Bad One exists, you do him credit!'

Jemmy grinned, taking this as a compliment.

'And if you was to fall in the water, I dare say you'd float. And if I was a shark, I wouldn't touch you. And if you got drownded, it'd be no loss to anybody. So far as I'm concerned, you can come. What about it, Thomas and Molly? The young 'un's right. He won't make much difference to what the canoe can carry.'

'Oh, I suppose he can come,' said Thomas reluctantly.

'Is it really so dangerous, Uncle Abel?' Molly asked.

'Course not, my dear,' said Abel confidently. 'Not on a calm sea, with an experienced man of sixty in charge!'

Chapter 8

BETH woke Molly before dawn on Prayer Day morning. After all her bad nights, Molly had slept soundly at last, now that she was doing something. It was Beth whose sleep was disturbed this time. Adam had agreed to join the trip to Kingfisher. With the help of Hester Reeves, a cover story had been concocted. Sheep were said to have strayed on to Slippery Edge, at the opposite end of the island, and Adam was taking Molly and Thomas to help him retrieve them. The Reader didn't really like anyone to be away on Prayer Day, but it was accepted that saving livestock from danger was sufficient reason.

'We'll have to leave before daylight and get back after dark,' Adam had said. 'Mustn't risk being seen.'

To Beth that was the least of the risks. If the expedition came to grief, she stood to lose brother, sister and lover all at once. And there would be no other husband for Beth; young men were few, since the loss of the boat Petrel four years earlier.

Molly sensed Beth's apprehension, but didn't share it.

'Don't worry!' she whispered, embracing her sister before creeping quietly from the house. 'We know what we're doing.'

'I hope,' she said to herself.

Adam and Thomas were waiting outside. Each carried a sack, holding such supplies as Hester Reeves and Adam's mother, Martha Goodall, had been able to spare. It seemed a pathetically small amount to take to a dozen people.

The sky was still cloudless, the moon just past full, and light was reflected from the sea in a million moving fragments. The upland was milky, the sheer cliffs beyond it sharp and black, and the houses of the village threw moon-shadows. No lamp shone from any of them and no dog barked as Adam, Molly and Thomas went barefoot by.

Last of all they passed the derelict house of Jonathan Wilde. The previous time Molly had walked past it she had felt nothing. This time the shudder down her spine was intensified by cold and excitement. She was living, dangerously. She wasn't sure that she liked it, but she wouldn't have wished it otherwise. And she was going to see Otipo again, she hoped. Her heart bumped. Otipo and, of course, Mua.

They'd hoped that when it came to the point Jemmy Kane wouldn't join them after all. But when they arrived at Abel's cave he was there already. He and Abel had stowed fishing gear and some of Abel's scanty stores in the canoe; and from the recesses of the cave Abel had produced two or three basic tools and a little timber, the scarcest of all resources on Halcyon. Together, all five of them pushed the boat out to the water's edge.

'I never heard the surf so quiet,' Thomas remarked.

'Maybe the Deliverer's on *our* side, eh?' said Abel. 'Or is it the Bad One?' He chuckled.

'You're a wicked old man,' said Thomas. 'Saying such things at your age. How old did you say you were? Fifty-five?'

'Twenty-one today!' declared Abel, and chuckled again. Jemmy's laugh rose high above his. Then, 'Come on, Moll, in you go! Jump for it, lass, if you're coming!'

Adam and Thomas paddled the canoe out through the gap in the reef.

'Sail up now?' Thomas asked.

'Not yet, lad,' said Abel. 'Not with a lee shore and all them rocks!'

They paddled for some time before Abel would let Thomas raise the sail. And then they were reaching: scudding swiftly to the south, past headland after ragged headland. Jemmy, without being told, moved surefooted on to the outrigger and balanced there so that Thomas could let out more sail.

Molly, with the spray sharp on her face, felt she'd lost touch with daily reality and was moving through a dream more vivid than waking life. Over to the east, a thin bar of yellow on the horizon told them it was almost dawn.

They were past the southernmost point of Halcyon now, but Abel wouldn't let Thomas turn westward until there was a broad expanse of clear water between the boat and the island. Then there was a lurch as Thomas took the canoe round through the wind, and they were reaching in the other direction, heading directly for Kingfisher. The breeze freshened and the sea creamed in their wake as the day came up behind them.

Halcyon dwindled rapidly, but for some time Kingfisher remained only a small dark hump on the horizon. All the world seemed sea now, and the boat was small, frail, unprotected. No one had anything to say. Molly, tired of watching in vain for any perceptible diminution in their distance from Kingfisher, tried turning away and scanning the sky, the seabirds, the sea behind them, the faces of her companions; and then looking suddenly forward again, hoping their goal would have drawn magically nearer. And still for a long time nothing seemed to happen, and all their swift progress to have no visible result.

In spite of her watchfulness, she was taken by surprise in the end; a moment came when she realized that it was day and the outline of Kingfisher was growing steadily closer and clearer. The looming volcanic cliffs — as high and sheer as Halcyon's — were all that could be seen at first, but as the light brightened and the distance narrowed, the beach and the patch of flatland at the near side of the island could be seen, and on it the tiny figures of people. Behind that flat patch, the rockface looked sheer and smooth as a wall.

'Drop the sail!' Abel told Thomas. 'There's a fringe of kelp here. We'll paddle over it.' And in a moment the sea beneath the canoe had become a reddish brown and was full of the wreathed and twisted branches of thick fleshy seaweed. It dragged at the base of the canoe, and Molly wondered if they would stick on it. Then they were over; and like a reef it enclosed a stretch of calm water, so that they could paddle quietly in toward the beach.

'There's only half of them here!' Thomas said. And indeed there were only six of the New People waiting for them: two men, three women and Mua. They stood in a half circle, keeping their distance as Adam and Thomas drew the canoe up on to the beach. Their faces were wary and unwelcoming.

'I don't suppose they expect any good from us,' Adam said. But when the Halcyon islanders went ashore and advanced with friendly signs and expressions, Mua broke the mould of reserve and ran forward.

'Ai-bell!' she cried. 'Toe-mass!' Laughing and weeping, she was embracing them all. The other five New People relaxed and smiled uncertainly, but still seemed puzzled.

'Where is Otipo?' Thomas asked at once.

Mua was obviously struggling for words with which to reply. She pointed to the rockface and made little climbing motions with her fingers before saying something to Thomas in her own language.

'What's she say, Thomas?' inquired Jemmy.

'I don't understand them as well as they understand us,' Thomas admitted. 'But I think she means the rest of them climbed the rockface and got to the other part of the island.'

'Climbed the rockface!' Abel was astonished. 'It don't hardly seem possible. I told you before, folk have died down here, not able to get off the flatland!'

'Climb.' Mua recognised the word and repeated it. 'They climb good.'

'I'll bet they do!' said Abel, impressed.

'And look!' said Molly. 'They've made themselves some shelter and a fire!'

So they had. Against the wall of rock, close by the point where a tiny spring emerged to make its way across flatland and beach into the sea, the New People had made themselves a kind of bower out of branches of the twisted, low-growing tree known on Halcyon as island oak. In front of it was a fire, and there was something cooking. Abel sniffed.

'Mollymauk,' he said. 'They been catching birds on top of those cliffs. They haven't just sat back, have they? They're doing better than I'd 'a' thought anyone could. But it's a desolate place, ain't it? I wouldn't like trying to live on Kingfisher.'

Then there were shouts and waves from the top of the cliff. Men and women shouted back from below. Half a dozen figures, one after the other, moved swiftly down the rockface, finding tiny fingerholds and toeholds, clinging precariously yet surely, and calling to each other and the people below as they came. The Halcyon islanders, though accustomed to skilful climbing, watched them with respect.

The first to reach beach level was Otipo. He ran across, his face breaking into a smile, and after bending a knee briefly to Mua he embraced the Halcyon islanders.

'My friends!' he declared.

Molly wondered whether he hugged her for a little longer than the others; wondered whether there was a special look for her in his eyes as he did so. Hester Reeves had been right in guessing that Molly didn't know she was in love. Molly wasn't used to analysing her emotions. She merely experienced them. When she saw Otipo she yearned for him and hoped he liked her.

'Come!' Otipo said. 'We give you to eat!'

The food was indeed mollymauk, or fulmar, cooked on a base of stones in its own plentiful fat.

'You're doing well, aren't you?' Thomas said with admiration.

'We live,' Otipo said. 'We catch birds, a few fish. And up there . . .' He pointed toward the high plateau above the cliff. 'Up there are other animals. We do not catch any yet, but we hope. We try. I do not know how you call them.'

'Goats?' said Thomas.

'Goats?' echoed Otipo doubtfully. 'I don't know.'

Thomas imitated the bleat of a goat. Otipo repeated it. They bleated to each other several times, laughing. Then Otipo broke off, his expression changing.

'But we are sad,' he said. 'On Rikofia we were so many people. Now we are so few. We think the others are all dead. And we have no home.'

'Rikofia,' said Abel thoughtfully. 'I'm sure I heard Grandad talk of Rikofia. It had something to do with us once, but I don't know what.' And then, sharply, 'You live now, but what about winter?'

Otipo and Thomas began a conversation in a mixture of both their languages, with frequent baffled breakings-off and shakings of heads. Then Thomas led the way back to the canoe, and the stores the Halcyon islanders had brought were unloaded. It didn't take long.

'Don't look very grateful, do they?' remarked Jemmy Kane.

'I don't see why they should be,' said Adam. 'It's little enough, after the way we treated them.'

There was plenty of interest in the nets, lines and fish-hooks, though, and the sheepskins and old clothes were received appreciatively. 'It is cold here at night, so cold,' Mua said, shrugging her way into an enormous seaman's jersey. And at last the other Rikofians began to smile and look friendly. Only the tall one whom they'd noticed standing aloof in the Meeting-House on Halcyon remained silently apart from the rest, looking thoughtfully at the canoe.

Jemmy hissed, in a thrilling, half-alarmed whisper, 'What if they was to murder us and take the boat? We ain't got no weapons.'

'They won't do that!' Abel said confidently. 'These folk aren't murderers. You only have to look at them to know that. I like 'em better than I do most of ours, I can tell you that!'

'Hey, Abel!' Thomas called. 'Adam! Molly! Listen to this! Otipo wants to take us to the other part of the island.'

'That's easier said than done,' Abel remarked. 'Unless you climb like a fly on a wall, the way these people do.'

'Wait a minute, wait a minute. You know why?'

'Why?'

'Because,' said Thomas, 'he says there's another man on the

far side of the island. Not a man like them. A man like us!'

'There ain't just *one* man!' said Abel. 'There's four. Harry and his lot. I been waiting for somebody to mention them. I been waiting for somebody to say, let's go and look for them. And if you want to know what I think, well, I think the less we have to do with them the better. Just leave 'em alone and let 'em go back to Halcyon in their own time. They'll tire of Kingfisher soon enough.'

'You got it wrong, Abel,' said Thomas. 'There's another one that we've never heard of before. A castaway or something.'

'That's right,' said Otipo. 'Another man. Sharlee.'

Everyone stared. Otipo tried to explain.

'Sharlee is not of your boat crew. Sharlee comes from ship that sink. He lives on Kingfisher two years. Your boat crew find Sharlee's house, stay one day, then go with guns to hunt . . .'

'Goats?' said Thomas.

'Yes, to hunt goats. Sharlee is glad they go, he does not like these men. He wishes they go back to Halcyon. I talk to Sharlee two times. I think he is good man.'

'Well!' said Abel. 'Two years on Kingfisher, and we never heard of him!'

'That's not surprising, is it?' said Adam. 'We don't come to Kingfisher. It's Sin Island, remember. If the Reader had his way, there'd be none of us on Kingfisher now.'

'Come!' said Otipo. 'Come and see Sharlee!' Then he looked doubtfully at Abel.

'Can climb, Uncle Abel?' he asked.

Abel shook his head as he looked at the cliff-face.

'Even when I was younger,' he said, 'I'd have thought that was a hard one. Mind you, if there was anyone on Halcyon in my young days who could 'a' done it, it'd have been me. There wasn't a climber on the island like Abel Oakes. Least of all William Jonas. But now, at my age . . . No, I think it'd be a bit too much for me.'

Otipo looked at Thomas. Molly saw in her brother's face the terror that the thought of climbing always brought on.

'Thomas has hurt his foot,' she said, trying desperately to find an excuse for him. And luckily Abel came to the rescue.

'Sea's still calm,' he said. 'Why don't we take the boat round? That's if there's anywhere to land. Ask him about it, Thomas.'

Thomas and Otipo talked again in a mixture of languages, with a great deal of gesture. Then Thomas said,

'If I got it right, there's a little beach, and this man has a hut close beside it. But Otipo says he has a gun.'

'That's right,' Otipo said. 'Sharlee has gun. Shoot animals.'

'What if he shoots *us*?' said Thomas.

'Why should he shoot us?' asked Abel, staring. 'We ain't no reason to think he's a cannibal, have we? If we go there unarmed, he'll see we're no danger to him. I want to find out who he is and what he's doing. Maybe him and these folk could get together and help each other.'

Thomas still looked doubtful. He spoke to Otipo again. Then he said, 'According to Otipo it's only a short distance by land over the cliff but it's quite a long way by sea. And this man may be alarmed if he sees more visitors in boats. It seems Harry and his crew found out he had liquor, and made a nuisance of themselves. He had a job to get rid of them.'

'Liquor!' said Molly, shocked. There was no liquor on Halcyon, and cautionary tales were told of its dire effects. Then a thought came to her.

'I can climb,' she said. 'Why don't Otipo and me go to this man by land? Then it won't take him by surprise when the boat comes.'

'He might be a rough character,' said Abel dubiously.

'And that cliff's enough to scare anyone,' said Thomas.

'I'm not frightened!' Molly declared. 'And if Otipo can get up that cliff, so can I!'

Otipo understood what she was suggesting, and unlike most Halcyon islanders he didn't seem to think it shocking that a girl should climb, or surprising that she should be able to. He beamed.

'Yes, Mol-lee, come!' he said, and took her hand. Molly's heart leaped.

'I can climb, too!' Jemmy piped up.

Molly found herself suddenly furious. She didn't want Jemmy to come. And perhaps Adam read her mind.

'*Oh*, no!' he said at once. 'You're coming in the boat with us, young Jemmy. I want you where I can keep an eye on you!'

'This way,' Otipo said to Molly. They set off up the cliff. Thomas watched from below with apprehension; he could never really believe that anyone was safe while climbing. But Molly followed Otipo with delight and exhilaration. He was surefooted and so was she. Neither of them could put a foot wrong; it was impossible. Every handhold felt friendly to her; every foothold seemed to welcome her feet. When she had to press her body to the cliff-face it was reassuringly solid. At one point there was a sidestep to be made which meant transferring her weight through the air. She didn't feel a moment's hesitation. Just now she knew her balance to be immaculate, her timing perfect, her movements beautifully precise, controlled, unfailing. She was as sure of herself as a bird on the wing. It seemed almost too soon when she was at the top and Otipo was hauling her on to the island's high rough plateau.

She stood, on more or less level ground, in front of Otipo. They were out of sight from the beach below. Exhilaration filled her whole being. She could do anything. She put her arms round Otipo, hugged him close to her, and was covering his face with kisses. And now she knew just what she felt.

'I love you!' she proclaimed triumphantly.

'I love you?' he repeated in a questioning tone. Molly took her face from his long enough to say 'Yes, I love you!' and then was kissing him again. It was Otipo who eventually broke it up, smiling.

'It is good, I-love-you,' he said; and then, 'You have no man?'

Molly put Dan Wilde straight out of her mind. She didn't want to think about Dan Wilde.

'No!' she declared. 'Only you!' And then, with sudden misgiving, 'You have a girl, Otipo? Is Mua your girl?'

The smile faded from Otipo's face.

'On our island, I had a girl,' he said. 'Now I have no island, no girl. Mua is not my girl. Mua . . .'

He struggled to put his meaning into words.

'We have, like you have Reader,' he said.

'A headman? Someone who tells you what to do?'

'Yes. Mua is child of him. But he is dead. So now we are people of Mua.'

Otipo smiled again, though the smile seemed a sad one. Molly, returning to earth after the exaltation of the climb, was appalled by her own forwardness. She blushed and turned away. And, far down on her right, she saw the canoe with the four tiny figures on board, setting off to round the headland. Otipo saw them in the same moment.

'Come,' he said. 'We go now.'

This part of Kingfisher was craggy upland. Over to their left was a peak, almost as high as the one on Halcyon, and between it and them was what looked like a chain of craters. Ahead was a ridge that formed a neck between two parts of the island. Otipo led the way toward it. For the moment he seemed to have forgotten the recent embrace, and Molly was still embarrassed. They moved steadily uphill. Seabirds wheeled, dipped and screamed around them.

Then they were on the ridge and looking down the other side. To a Halcyon islander, it was like being on the far side of the moon. The side of Kingfisher which presented itself to Halcyon was familiar; the other side was something new. And it wasn't quite like Halcyon itself. True, there were the steep, stacked cliffs, alive with millions of birds. But where a stream ran down there was a thin winding band of green. Molly's eyes followed it down and came to a patch of tilled ground, an inlet, a tiny beach of black sand through which the stream ran out to sea. In a sheltered space beside the inlet was a hut with a chimney, from which rose a wisp of smoke.

And drawn up beside it was a boat. It looked like a Halcyon island boat.

'It's *Seamew*!' Molly exclaimed. 'Harry's boat!'

'The men! They have come back!' Otipo frowned. 'Sharlee did not wish them back.'

'Whatever's happening?' Molly asked. But there could be no answer to that. Otipo shook his head.

'Come on!' Molly said. 'We better go and see!'

They made for the stream and followed it down the hillside. Though not as difficult as the cliff, it was an awkward descent. There was no path, and from time to time the stream took a downward leap and became a steep narrow waterfall. They scrambled down as best they could, and were thankful to reach the bottom without mishap. The patch of tilled land at which they arrived was neat, levelled and weeded, and there were rows of potatoes, peas, carrots and beetroot.

The hut itself appeared to be made mostly from ships' timbers. From it came a smell of cooked meat. And as they drew near, Molly noticed another smell: a smell half-recognised, at once seductive and disturbing. From inside the hut came sounds of rough, raised voices, and one of them burst into a raucous, out-of-tune song.

Molly felt apprehensive, though at first she didn't quite know why. She knew the voices, and her ear quickly distinguished between them. There were the thin sharp abrasive tones of Harry Kane, the low thick ones of Bob Attwood, the strange accent of Alec Campbell which had come down in his family from long ago, and at one point the braying laugh of lumpish Len Wilde, who was generally thought to be as slow-witted as Luke Jonas and a good deal less amiable.

Molly had known the owners of these voices ever since she could remember, and though she disliked Harry and Bob she had never been afraid of them. But there was a difference today; it had something to do with that strange, heady smell, and it made her uneasy.

She and Otipo crouched by the back of the hut. No

window overlooked them. The obvious thing would have been to go to the front and make their presence known; but Molly was reluctant to do so, and sensed that Otipo felt as she did.

'What are we going to do?' she whispered to him.

Otipo hesitated. He seemed about to reply when a door slammed and a man came round the side of the hut, heading for the pile of firewood nearby. He stopped short on seeing Otipo and Molly; then after a moment said quietly, 'Teepo! And who's this?'

The man was a stranger: apart from the incomers the only stranger Molly had seen since she was a little girl.

'I'm Molly Reeves, sir,' she said, and blushed.

'You don't 'sir' me,' the man said. He was heavily built and was in late middle age. He had a reddish face, very blue eyes, thick curly grey eyebrows, a massive grey beard and a much smaller amount of grey hair. He wore a blue seaman's jersey, but his trousers were clumsily home-made of sealskin.

'I'm Charlie Herrick,' he told her, 'one-time mate of the *Lydia*, and now my own skipper as you might say, though this hut is all the ship I have, and just now she's been boarded. Those fellers have come back, Teepo. I was afraid they would.' He looked at Molly with some curiosity.

'Where do you come from, Molly?' he inquired. 'I been over two years on this island, and until the other day I never saw a soul. Can't say I wanted to, particularly. And now all of a sudden there's this precious crew that's claiming to be great pals of mine, and drinking my liquor on the strength of it, and there's *your* folk, Teepo, and now *you*, Molly. What's going on?'

'I'm from Halcyon,' Molly said. 'There's four more of us. The others are coming round the headland now.'

Charlie pulled a face.

'Not more like these, I hope!'

'Not like them at all!' Molly declared with feeling.

'P'raps your lot are coming to take these back to Halcyon?' Charlie suggested hopefully.

'Not really. We came to help the New People. Otipo and his friends.'

'Aye, well, I can tolerate *them*,' Charlie said. 'Me and Teepo's got to know each other, these last few days. We gets on well together, even if we don't always understand what's being said. But these fellers that's in my house now, they're a different kettle of fish.' He dropped his voice. 'Listen, Molly. They're drunk, you understand? Early in the day as it is, they're drunk. Later on they'll be helpless, and *then* old Charlie's going to deal with them. But just now, Molly, it ain't no place for a girl. You get down to the beach with Teepo here, and make sure your own folk pick you up. You can leave the others to me.'

But there was no time for Molly to get away. A man came reeling round the side of the hut, and saw them at once. It was heavy, shambling Bob Attwood. Usually Bob was the worst-tempered man on Halcyon. But now a beaming smile spread over his bristly face.

'Why, i'ss Molly!' he pronounced. He peered for a moment as if in temporary doubt, then said, 'Yes, 'course i'ss Molly. Big lovely Molly!' He lurched toward her. Molly backed away, but not quickly enough. Bob held her in a ponderous embrace. The reek of his breath in her face was unbearable.

'That'll do, Bob,' said Charlie Herrick. 'The young lady don't like it.'

To Molly's surprise, Bob let her go at once.

'If you say so, Charlie,' he said with exaggerated respect. 'You're our host, ain't you? We're your guests. Your honoured guests. Molly me dear, me and my friends is the guests of the King of Kingfisher, Cap'n Charlie Herrick. And who's this? One of the savages! Why you mixing with the savages, Molly? I recognise this one. He's the good-looking lad that stayed with old Abel, ain't he? Oh, Molly, Molly, what you up to?'

Molly didn't deign to reply. She said to Charlie, 'I could have shook him off, you know. I'm not scared of Bob Attwood.'

Bob seized Otipo's hand in his own massive paw.

'Shake hands, savage!' he said. 'I got nothing against savages, so long as they ain't on Halcyon. And come on in, both of you. Our host wants you to come into his house, don't you, Charlie?'

'Don't go in. Run for it!' Charlie advised Molly, tersely. But Bob dropped Otipo's hand and grabbed Molly's. And a moment later the other three members of *Seamew*'s crew, two of them with glasses in their hands, had staggered out into the open. Molly and Otipo were surrounded, and were nudged gently but insistently, amid expressions of welcome and enthusiasm, into the main room of Charlie's hut.

Chapter 9

To Molly's eyes, Charlie Herrick's dwelling seemed luxuriously equipped. The floor was boarded and had a rug on it. There were four plain oak chairs and an upholstered armchair. On a handsome polished table was an elaborate brass oil-lamp; items of plate shone from a wooden dresser that stood against a wall. Most remarkable of all, there were several rows of leather-bound books, like smaller versions of the Book in the Meeting-House on Halcyon.

But the brief occupancy of the *Seamew* crew had already made the room look disordered. There was a pool of liquor on the floor; a book lay open in it, face down; used plates and a blackened pan sat on the beautiful polished surface of the table.

The armchair was clearly the seat of honour, and Harry Kane lowered himself into it.

'Well, we're all glad to see you, Molly!' he declared. There was an incongruous cordiality in his thin, grating voice. 'Your good health, Moll, that's what us drinking folk say!' He raised a glass to his lips, drank, and spluttered.

'And *your* health, savage!' said Bob.

Len, who was the most helplessly drunk of them all, giggled wildly and sank to a squatting position in a corner, where the wall gave his back some support. As he did so, the glass fell from his hand and broke.

'Careful, careful, Len,' said Harry. 'That was clumsy. No way to treat Charlie's property. Even Charlie don't have *that* many glasses, and he can't replace 'em. You can't buy glasses on Kingfisher like as if you was in London, can you, Charlie?'

Len Wilde gave another witless giggle.

'You see, Molly,' Harry went on, 'our host's a much travelled man. That's right, ain't it, Charlie? You're a much travelled man. Been to London and Bristol and America and Deliverer-knows-where. Don't put your hand in that broken glass, Len, you tater-head. Get up and fetch the young lady a drink. Port wine for her, I should think. Eh, Molly? That's what ladies drinks in the Outside World, I'm told, and Charlie's got a couple o' cases of it in that outhouse.'

'Len's in no fit state to fetch onnything,' said long-faced Alec Campbell.

'Then fetch it yourself, Alec!' said Harry. 'And don't forget your friends. And what about our host? You ain't drinking, Charlie. Don't you want to celebrate?'

'I got nothing to celebrate,' said Charlie.

'Come, come, Charlie, don't talk like that!' Harry said reproachfully. 'A lovely wreck like you had, with all that timber, and enough supplies for years! You've rebuilt the captain's cabin right here in this house, ain't you? Made a good job of it, too. It's comfortable. And the drink, Charlie, the drink!'

'It won't last for ever, the rate you're getting through it!' said Charlie.

Len's laughter rang out again.

'The only thing you was short of till now,' Harry said, 'was company. And now you got company. You got us. And when we go — though we ain't in no hurry, Charlie, you'll be glad to know — you'll still have the savages, won't you? You can teach 'em to read them books!' Harry laughed. 'Hey, Alec, this savage ain't got a drink. A drink for the savage! What'll you drink, savage? Rum or brandy?'

Otipo shook his head.

'He don't understand,' said Bob Attwood. 'He's only a savage. You want some rum, savage? RUM? Here, try it!' He shoved his glass under Otipo's nose. Otipo turned away. Bob was offended. 'Don't you refuse my kindness, savage!' he warned Otipo.

'Now, now, Bob, we're all friends here!' said Harry. 'I reckon Charlie wouldn't like it if there was to be any trouble.

And Charlie's the one that matters round here. Our host! Time we drank his health again. Hurry up, Alec, there's empty glasses here!'

Alec returned with a jug, from which he slopped liquor into three glasses. He looked down at Len with contempt. 'You'll get more when you can come for it!' he said. Len grinned foolishly. Under his arm Alec had a bottle.

'That's vintage port,' said Harry. 'A glass of port, Molly, my dear. Be a woman of the world. Don't you want to try it?'

'I ain't curious,' said Molly. She added virtuously, 'Drink's sinful, isn't it? That's the Teaching.'

'The Teaching!' said Harry. 'You're on Sin Island now, Molly, me girl. The Teaching don't count for nothing here! Only one thing counts here, and that's being friends and having a good time. And, Molly, you can't have come over from Halcyon on your own! Who's with you? Has William Jonas sent for us?'

'There's Adam Goodall and Abel Oakes and Thomas,' said Molly. 'And your son. Jemmy.'

'Oh, Jemmy's here, is he?' Harry said. He didn't sound too pleased.

'Poor wee laddie!' said Alec Campbell, with drunken solemnity. 'I feel sorry for Jemmy. He's fonder of you than you are of him, Harry!'

'That'll do, Alec,' said Harry. 'We get enough preaching from the Reader. Let me tell you, I got natural feelings same as anyone else. I love that boy, love him dearly. But there's times when a dad don't necessarily want his lad to be around.' He turned to Molly.

'You've come from Halcyon in the other boat, I suppose. *Shearwater*. But it don't sound like much of a crew to me. Three youngsters and an old feller like Abel. There's only Adam that's fit to be sent on a man's errand. Why didn't William pick a proper crew? And where are they all now?'

'C'mon, Harry! Don't start getting serious!' urged Bob. 'You're as bad as Alec. Drink up!'

'We're not in *Shearwater*,' Molly said. 'We're in the canoe that Otipo and Mua arrived in. And it'll be coming round the headland any minute.'

'It will, eh?' said Harry thoughtfully. He got up and made his way to the window. 'I don't see no sign of it now. They got any weapons, Molly?'

'No.'

'They're no match for us, then. They couldn't make us go back if they tried.'

'We didn't set out to make you go back,' Molly said.

'Maybe not. Anyway, you can take a message back to William Jonas. You can tell him we'll be returning to Halcyon if and when we feel like it. Our friend Charlie has plenty of food, and with a bit of luck we'll add to it with a goat now and then. We didn't have much luck with the shooting yesterday, I admit, but I guess we're all out of practice.'

'That's what you call it, Harry! I'd say we're drunk!' said Alec Campbell, in a tone suggesting strong disapproval of any such condition. He drank again.

'Between you and me and old Charlie there,' Harry said to Molly, 'if we do go back in the end, it'll have been worth it, whatever trouble we're in. And, Molly me dear, why don't you stay with us and join the fun?'

'Ah, now you're talking!' Bob Attwood said. Molly was aware that he was eyeing her up and down. Of all the group, she liked the look of Bob least.

'I'm not staying with *you* lot!' she declared stoutly.

Alec Campbell went round again with the jug. Harry Kane called from the window, 'Here they are! Coming in to land! Come on, fellers, we'll go down and meet them. And bring the guns, just in case!'

With Bob and Alec he set off for the beach. Molly and Charlie, temporarily forgotten, went and stood at the window. Otipo joined them. The three men went first into an outhouse, from which they emerged carrying muskets.

'I reckon those are ready to fire,' Charlie said in a worried tone. 'And I don't like it. There's no telling what might happen. I seen fellers before when the rum starts talking in them. When you got drunken men with loaded guns, there's as much danger from accidents as from anything they actually mean to do. Now, let's go and meet your friends. And, Molly, keep eyes all round your head, watch me as well as the rest, and trust old Charlie. I been in much worse situations than this, and I don't want no trouble, but if there *is* trouble I mean to come out on top!'

The canoe was just landing when Molly and Otipo followed Charlie to the beach. Adam and Thomas leaped ashore and dragged it up. Harry Kane, who had put his musket down on a flat stone, came forward and helped them.

'Dad!' called Jemmy Kane. 'Dad!' He jumped from the boat and ran to his father.

'Hello, son,' Harry said. He embraced Jemmy for a brief moment, then pushed him aside. 'Gimme a moment, lad, I'm busy just now.' Jemmy stood outraged with open mouth, but Harry didn't notice.

'What you think you're doing here?' he asked the new arrivals. 'You got permission from the King of Kingfisher?' And, as everyone looked bewildered, Harry laughed his grating laugh. '*That's* the King of Kingfisher,' he said. 'Our host. Cap'n Herrick. We're his guests. And take a look each side of you.'

Adam and Thomas were already looking from side to side. Alec Campbell and Bob Attwood raised their guns to their shoulders. The muzzles wavered uncertainly.

'Put them things down!' said Charlie, 'You'll be hurting somebody!'

The muskets were lowered. Harry said to Adam, 'You've come at an awkward time. We're having a party. It's a good party. A very good party. But you ain't been invited.'

'*I'm* inviting them,' said Charlie Herrick.

'No, no, Charlie. You're a generous feller, we all know. But we don't want you wasting good liquor on this lot. Now, Adam, you got anything to say to us before you go?'

'Not much,' Adam said. 'The Reader wants you back, but he didn't send us to fetch you. He doesn't know we've come.'

'Well, you can take him a message,' said Harry. 'Give him

our compliments and say we'll come when we're good and ready.'

'That's all right with me,' Adam said. 'I've got no authority over you. Just let Molly on board, and we'll be away.'

'Let Molly on board?' repeated Harry Kane. 'Well, now, that's another matter. Molly *has* been invited. She's having a good time, aren't you, love?'

'No,' said Molly.

'We'll keep Molly with us for a while, if you don't mind,' Harry said. 'For company. As for Jemmy, well, it's nice to have seen him, but I reckon you can take him away again. He's in good hands, I don't doubt.'

'Dad!' protested Jemmy, agonised. 'You can't do that! Dad!'

'This ain't no place for children,' Harry said. 'This is Sin Island!'

Adam moved forward. Bob Attwood raised his gun again.

'You get back, Adam Goodall!' he roared. 'Watch it, or you'll be shot. I never settled matters with you the other day!'

'Come on, Molly,' Adam said. 'And Otipo, if you wish.'

'*Any* of you move, and you'll be shot!' bellowed Bob. His short spell of cordiality was over now. His heavy sullen face was enraged. He had hated Adam for years.

'There, there, Bob,' said Harry. 'That ain't going to be necessary. They're going to behave reasonable, I know. They don't want to be harmed, any more than we wants to harm them.'

But Adam was getting provoked now.

'I'll settle matters with you any time you like, Bob Attwood!' he declared. 'Fists, not guns! He stepped forward again. And a shot rang out.

Everyone was shaken. Nobody knew where the bullet went. It didn't hit anyone. Nobody knew at first where it came from, either. Bob Attwood, who hadn't fired, lowered his gun and looked at it as if in disbelief. Then, all at once, everybody saw Len Wilde, who had staggered unnoticed from Charlie's outhouse with a musket, fired wildly, and been pushed over backward by the recoil.

At that moment Charlie Herrick acted, swiftly and neatly. He grabbed Bob's gun by the muzzle, wrenched it from him, and felled him instantly with a blow to the head. Alec Campbell, dazed and three parts drunk, lurched forward, lost his footing, and fired unintentionally into the sand. In a moment Otipo was on his back and Thomas tackling him round the legs. Charlie moved rapidly round and knocked Alec in turn on the head. Adam leaped at Harry Kane, who dodged a blow and fought back. They grappled with each other. Charlie darted in and laid Harry out as calmly as if he'd been swatting a fly.

'Well, that's that,' he said. 'Takes better men than them by a long chalk to beat Charlie. I'd have dealt with 'em before long whether you'd come or not. I just had to deal with 'em a bit sooner, that's all.'

Then a small whirlwind launched itself at Charlie. It was Jemmy Kane, head down, fists flying. 'You bastard!' Jemmy yelled. 'What you done to my dad?'

Charlie held him off with one brawny arm.

'You're a terror, aren't you?' he said. 'Best man of the lot of them, I reckon.' After a final flurry of useless blows, Jemmy collapsed, sobbing. Charlie put an arm round him. 'There, there,' he said, 'your dad'll be all right.'

'We haven't killed any of them?' Adam inquired anxiously.

'Course not,' said Charlie. 'I'd have hit 'em harder if I'd been killing 'em. They'll come round all too soon. Now, wait a moment while I get some rope, and I'll give you a lesson in how to tie knots.'

But Charlie's handling of rope was too deft for the eyes of the others to follow. In a few minutes Harry, Bob and Alec were tightly and expertly trussed.

'Now,' said Charlie, 'why don't you all come into Charlie's hut? You can do with something to drink, and maybe to eat.' Then his eye fell on Thomas.

'What's the matter with him?' he asked.

Thomas, weak-kneed with shock, was being held up by Molly and Otipo. 'It's just the — the violence,' he said feebly. 'I never seen anything like this before. We don't have violence on Halcyon.'

'This ain't Halcyon,' said Abel Oakes. 'This is Sin Island.'

Len Wilde had staggered back into the hut and collapsed on the floor, where he lay snoring. Charlie shoved him out of the way, produced a shovel and quickly swept up broken glass. He flung the door and the two windows wide.

'That'll get rid of the smell,' he said. 'Now, make yourselves at home. It never rains but what it pours, does it? The last two years, I been within a few miles of Halcyon, and never saw nobody from there. Didn't even know for sure it *was* Halcyon, not having no charts, but I reckoned it must be. How many folks is there living on the island now?'

'About a hundred,' said Adam.

'Aye. Seems a lot to me these days, seeing I'm not used to company. But I'm not surprised. I seen their boats from time to time, but I don't think they've ever seen *me*. Is that right?'

'That's right.'

'They don't come around here, or didn't till the other day. I wonder why not.'

'It's the Teaching,' Molly told him. 'We aren't supposed to come to Kingfisher. The Deliverer sent folk here that was possessed by the Bad One, and it's in the Book that we're to keep away from sin. Like Uncle Abel said, this is Sin Island.'

An alarming thought crossed her mind.

'Do you . . . belong to the Bad One?' she asked.

Charlie Herrick roared with laughter.

'That's rich,' he said. 'Me belong to the Bad One? Well, if I do, you had the Bad One on your side just now, didn't you? But I don't think so, somehow. Him and me haven't met, so far as I know. Now, who's hungry? Have some breakfast? I got plenty of food. What about you, Teepo? Breakfast?'

'Breakfast,' repeated Otipo. 'To eat. Yes, Sharlee, I like to eat.'

Molly looked at him and wanted to run her fingers down the smooth golden skin of his arm.

It seemed that everyone was hungry. Charlie put pieces of mollymauk in a huge pan on the fire, and it began to spit and sizzle in its own fat.

'Well, I'd rather have you here than *that* lot,' he remarked. 'Though, to tell you the truth, I don't need folk. Not really. Fact is, I'm quite happy here, retired as you might say, with my books to read and my own thoughts and my little friends.'

'Your little friends?' Molly echoed.

'Yes. You ain't noticed them? Oh well, I suppose there's been so much happening here, you've not had time to look around. See in that corner over there, there's two cages, one on top of the other. Go on, go and have a look.'

Thomas, who'd recovered now, went with Molly to the corner of the hut. There were two big metal boxes, with grids on the front. There seemed at first to be nothing in either of them except a tangle of dried grasses, but as Molly approached a group of little animals appeared from the back of the upper box. They had grey glossy fur, bright eyes and whiskers.

'I haven't seen mice this big before,' Molly said.

'Mice?' Charlie laughed heartily. 'Those ain't mice, my dear. Those is rats. The only survivors from the Lydia, exceptin' myself. I saved their lives. Well, strictly speaking it was their parents' lives I saved, but I've given these the same names. This one that's a bit on the browny side, that's Napoleon. And next to him, that's Blucher. The very dark one is Nelson, and behind him, that's Wellington. Those are the gents, you understand. I keeps the ladies separate. Them in the other cage is Emma and Josephine and Caroline and Sophia.'

He raised a catch, opened the upper box a fraction, and with a swift neat gesture pulled out Napoleon and closed the box again. Napoleon sat comfortably in his hand.

'They know Charlie won't hurt them,' said Charlie. 'I talks to them for hours. I like talking to them better than I ever did to sailors. They're less quarrelsome and never get drunk.

That's right, isn't it, Nappy old man? Want to hold him, me dear?'

'No, thank you,' said Molly, shuddering.

'He won't bite you, dear. They're all tame. Intelligent, too. You don't have rats on Halcyon, then?'

'No, we have mice.'

'Mice are poor creatures. They're nothing, compared with rats. Though I must say, it's just as well you don't have rats, I was on Tahiti once, and they have rats, and a great menace they are. If I was to let my little friends loose together, they'd soon be everywhere. Rats breed like nobody's business. And rats eat what *you* eat, me dear.'

Molly recoiled.

'So I keeps 'em behind bars, as you might say. I don't take no chances. Never have more than one of them out of the cage at once, just in case they was to get away. And now, talking of eating, I reckon our breakfast's ready. Let's close them windows and put some more wood on the fire and settle down, nice and cosy.'

'You're very comfortable here, Charlie, aren't you?' Adam said between mouthfuls a few minutes later.

'Aye. I'm a lucky feller. I tell myself so, often. Mind you, it still hurts me to think of how the *Lydia* went down. All them good men drowned, and only me spared. It makes you think, that does. I asks myself sometimes, "What was you spared for, Charlie?"'

'Maybe you were spared to help *us*,' Thomas suggested.

Charlie grinned.

'I ain't entering into the arguments behind *that* remark, young man!' he said. 'Maybe I'm just a natural survivor. But anyway, here I am, set up as it seems for the rest of my life, with my own billet, food for the taking, and all the stuff I got from the wreck. I did well from the poor old *Lydia*. Robinson Crusoe hardly did better. I got guns ashore, and enough powder for years. And taters and roots from the galley; I planted them and they all grew, the climate's kind to 'em here. And then there's the things I took from the captain's cabin. I knew old Cap'n Bowyer wouldn't be needing 'em no more; I seen him floating past me, dead. That's his silver plate that you're eating off now; and most of what's in this room, and all them books, they was all his.'

'You've read all those books, Charlie?' Thomas asked, marvelling.

'Most of 'em two or three times,' said Charlie. 'And I saved all the ship's instruments. Chronometer, quadrant, sextant, compass — I got them all, and I know how to use 'em. And liquor: I don't know how much rum and brandy I have in my store-room, in spite of what them fellers drank and spilt. Not that I *need* liquor. I don't often drink, I seen too much of what it does to folks, but I like to have a nightcap now and then.'

'You seen a lot of the world, ain't you, Charlie?' asked Abel. 'I expect you know London, eh?'

'Oh aye, I know London. And Bristol and Liverpool and New York and San Francisco and Singapore . . .'

The Halcyon islanders looked at Charlie with awe. They had heard the names of these great ports, but no one from Halcyon had been to any of them, and only Abel had ever even spoken to anyone who had.

'They do say London's a great sight,' he remarked.

'Aye, that's true. To go up the river at night, with scores of ships, and hundreds of lights shining everywhere — oh, it's a wonder of the world. And to walk in the streets, with thousands of people, and carriages wherever you go, and great buildings reaching up to the sky . . . But for all that, I don't think I want to see it again. I've had enough of cities.'

'Tell us some more about yourself,' said Thomas, fascinated. 'How did the ship come to be wrecked? Where had you sailed from?'

But Charlie hadn't much interest in his own story.

'It's not how I came to be here that matters,' he said. 'It's what I'm going to do now. I'd settled down to being on my own. And now there's Otipo and his friends here, and all you lot knowing about me. It's a bit unsettling.'

'Is there a living for twelve people on Kingfisher besides you?' Adam asked him.

'Well . . .' Charlie hesitated. 'They *might* just manage.

But if I was them, I'd try to get away before winter. It won't be too easy living here when the weather's bad and the birds is all gone. I got enough food for one; I ain't got enough for a dozen.'

'The fact is,' said Adam, 'we still need to get the New People back to Halcyon. And I still don't see how we'll do it.'

Len Wilde, who'd lain snoring in a corner of the room, now stirred, stopped snoring for a moment, rolled over and began to snore again.

'And right now,' Adam went on, 'we have to decide what to do with Harry and this lot.'

'You're in charge, Adam,' said Abel. 'But if I was you, I'd put 'em all aboard *Seamew* and take 'em back to William Jonas.'

'Well, I certainly don't want 'em here!' said Charlie Herrick.

'And how'll we get the canoe back to Halcyon as well?' asked Thomas.

'Ad-dam,' said Otipo. 'You want to help my people?'

'Of course, I do,' Adam said.

'Then give to my people the canoe. It is good to fish and go to the other side of the island.'

'When you come to think of it, Adam,' said Thomas, 'it's their canoe, isn't it? What right have we to keep it anyway?'

'None at all,' Adam said instantly. 'I hadn't thought about that.'

'Let's go back to where the New People are and hand the canoe over,' Thomas suggested. 'Then we can set off back to Halcyon. This trip can't be kept secret now, so we might as well try to get home in daylight.'

Adam bent over and hauled Len to his feet. Len stared around him, glassy-eyed and bewildered. 'Take his other arm, Thomas,' Adam said. And then, 'Good-bye, Charlie. Thank you for everything. Maybe we'll be meeting again.'

'Maybe,' said Charlie. 'Though I'm not one for social comings and goings, you know. Not really.'

'I know how you feel, Charlie,' Abel said. 'I been living alone for half a lifetime, and I wouldn't change it, not for anything except being married to a good girl, like I was when I was young. But I reckon you and me's past the time when we can hope for that!'

'I suppose so,' said Charlie ruefully. Molly felt a little wave of affection, and put her arms round him.

'Good-bye, Charlie!' she said softly. 'It was good of you to look after us so well. I'm glad you're a survivor.'

'Good-bye, me dear,' said Charlie. 'If folk were all like you, I'd like 'em better.' There was warmth in the grin he gave her. But as she went out she looked round and saw him cross to his shelves and pick up a book. She suspected that he wasn't sorry to be relieved of human company. His little friends watched from their cages.

'You can untie our hands now, Adam,' said Harry Kane, when the canoe had been returned to the New People and *Seamew* was on her way back to Halcyon. 'We won't try nothing. And it ain't exactly friendly, keeping your old pals tied up like this.'

'We untied your feet. Be thankful for that,' Adam said coldly. And for a while Harry made no further plea. He had other problems. The wind was rising, the sea was choppy, and he was feeling the effects of liquor and a blow on the head. He and Alec Campbell were sick over the gunwale; Len, looking ill and miserable, lay huddled in the bow. Only Bob Attwood sat glowering and apparently unaffected by anything except resentment.

When land was in sight and he was feeling better, Harry renewed his appeal. 'Fact is,' he said, 'you don't have no *right* to tie us up. You don't have no right to do anything like that unless the Reader tells you.'

'We'll see what he says when we arrive,' said Adam. 'Meanwhile, I'm taking no chances.'

'Oh, come on, Adam,' said Harry. 'Everyone's always been good pals on Halcyon, let's not spoil it. And listen, if you untie us, we can tell the Reader we came back voluntary. We'll say we was going to shoot a goat or two, so's we could bring back meat for everyone. As a matter of fact, that's the truth, more or less. It was just unlucky we didn't get any.'

'It was lucky you didn't shoot each other by accident, more likely!' said Abel Oakes scornfully.

Harry made an attempt at jauntiness. 'It's a kindness to the Reader not to upset him with tales of fighting and all that,' he said. 'Poor old feller. He'll be happier if he doesn't know.'

'Whatever we said, he'd know about the liquor,' Thomas remarked. 'He'd *smell* you.'

'The smell's wearing off,' said Harry. 'Anyway, William won't know what it is.'

'Oh yes he will,' said Adam. 'Sailors came ashore with liquor in the old days, when ships called. William Jonas'll know that smell all right. And he'll know what's wrong with Len. It's no good, Harry, I'm not going to budge. You'll have to stay like that. You brought it on yourselves.'

'And I always thought you was a nice feller, Adam Goodall,' said Harry reproachfully. Bob Attwood, seeing that Adam wasn't going to give way, swore at him ferociously and lapsed into scowling silence.

Seamew had been seen while still far out from Halcyon, and by the time she arrived at the landing-place the Reader and half the islanders were waiting. When she shot in, riding the surf, ready hands seized her gunwales and dragged her ashore. There was general astonishment as Harry, Bob and Alec, hands still bound, stepped awkwardly on to the beach. Harry wore a grin, as if to suggest that it was all a great joke. Bob scowled more fiercely than ever; Alec's face was lugubrious. Len had to be carried ashore by Molly and Thomas.

'*Now* what's been going on?' the Reader demanded.

Adam told the story, briefly and plainly. The Reader looked doubtful at first. His instructions had been disobeyed on all sides, and he was half inclined to discipline the captors as well as the captives. But a stop had been put to Harry's venture, and *Seamew* had been brought back to Halcyon safe and sound. And the Reader, like most of the bystanders, wasn't sorry to see Harry and Bob humiliated. He hesitated only for a moment. Then,

'Well done, lad, well done!' he declared, patting Adam on the back. 'You're a lad after me own heart. Just the way I'd have handled it when I was your age!' He turned to Jacob Wilde.

'You see, Jacob,' he said, 'there's some as knows what to do, and there's some as doesn't. Me and Adam's the first kind. You're the second kind, Jacob, you got to face it. You ain't the same calibre!'

'That's not quite fair,' Adam said. 'As I told you just now, it was mostly Charlie Herrick that dealt with the trouble. I didn't do anything that Jacob wouldn't have done in my place.'

'Now, now,' the Reader said, displeased. 'Don't spoil the occasion. I'm praising you in public, Adam Goodall, and my praise is not easily won, so I'll be glad if you'll value it. And now, I got to teach this precious crew a lesson!'

He addressed the delinquents sternly.

'Harry!' he said. 'You're the helmsman of *Seamew*, and the ringleader. It's only right you should be punished most. I'm going to have the lockup reopened, and you'll be put in it for a month to think about your wicked ways. And I hope you'll come out of it a better man!'

The thought of a month in the little damp lockup, unused in years, couldn't be a pleasant one. But Harry, putting a brave face on things, managed a thin-lipped smile.

'Thank you, Reader,' he said.

'As for the other three of you,' the Reader went on, 'you'll spend a week each in turn sitting all morning in the stocks, and working all afternoon in other folk's plots. If we wasn't short of men I'd remove you all from the *Seamew* crew, but I reckon that ain't possible. So you're getting off lightly. If you get a bit of rubbish thrown at you while you're in the stocks, it'll serve you right!'

'Nobody better throw anything at *me*!' growled Bob, 'or I'll make 'em sorry afterwards!'

'*Two* weeks in the stocks for you, Bob!' said the Reader promptly. 'Say one more word and it'll be three!' And Bob Attwood was silent.

Third Wave

SUMMER *fades into autumn, and Halcyon enters a season of deep unease. The escapade of Harry Kane and his crew, and the drama of their return in disgrace, seem to many islanders an alarming breach with their peaceable way of life. And as the first shock of the affair dies down, the thought of the New People's banishment re-emerges in people's minds and troubles many consciences, even among those who voted for it. The dark humped shape of Kingfisher on the horizon is a constant reminder of both these episodes; and always there is fear of the winter ahead. Even islanders who do not take the Bad One too seriously have a disturbing sense that a dark cloud lies over Halcyon.*

The scandal of Seamew *is followed swiftly by another. Widowed Cathy Oakes is observed by the island women to be growing stout at a rate which can suggest only one thing. The day comes when she has to acknowledge that she will soon be a mother for the fourth time. Her husband has been dead for three years. Sent for by the Reader to account for this situation, Cathy blames Harry Kane.*

Harry, now released from the lock-up, admits responsibility and seems rather proud of himself. He offers to make Cathy an honest woman, remarking that her children could do with a father and his Jemmy with a mum. But Cathy shocks the whole community by declaring that she won't marry Harry at any price. Pressure is put on her by the Reader, the elders and her neighbours, but she is immovable. Old Abel Oakes, her uncle by marriage, supports her, insisting that it is better for a child to be a bastard than to be brought up by Harry Kane.

Harry takes this badly. His rejection humiliates him more than his punishment had done. The Reader also takes it badly, especially as his granddaughter Abby, who has been growing up without his noticing the fact, asserts her independence and sides with Cathy. Moreover, Abby develops an affection for William's old enemy Abel, and frequently joins Molly and Thomas in trips to the cave to see him.

Bob Attwood meanwhile grows ever more bad-tempered, and utters threats of violence to several islanders. One night Cathy, now nearing her time, is assaulted from behind and has a bucket of filth thrown over her. A couple of days later, Thomas is caught on his own by Bob near the vegetable plots, and beaten up. The next day Dick Reeves fights Bob, loses, and is savagely kicked while lying on the ground. It is Bob's turn to spend time in the lock-up, and it takes half a dozen men to get him there.

Halcyon has never known such goings-on, and does not like them. Some say the Reader has treated Harry and Bob too harshly; others that he has not been harsh enough. Some are uneasy about the banishment of the New People; others blame them anew for each successive trouble. Some see Cathy Oakes as a heroine, others as a threat to the fabric of society. The whole island is at odds with itself. The Reader is visibly unhappy, and seems to be ageing rapidly as the days shorten and the hungry winter draws nearer.

Chapter 10

ONE afternoon in early autumn, Adam was met on his return from fishing with the news that the Reader wanted to see him. The Council of Elders had met earlier that day. In the evening Adam came round to the Reeveses' house in a state of mingled excitement and shock.

'Well, what did William want?' asked Dick Reeves.

'He's finding the present troubles too much to cope with. He says there hasn't been such disorder on Halcyon in all his life-time. He doesn't know what he did wrong, but he thinks the Bad One is winning.'

'And he called you in to tell you that?'

'He . . . he reckons he might retire as Reader and let someone else take over. He's tired.'

'Who would the somebody else be?' asked Hester sharply.

'Well . . . it'll surprise you.'

There was a silence, then Hester said,

'Maybe it won't surprise me.'

'Oh, Adam!' said Beth. 'It's not . . .?'

'Yes,' said Adam. 'It's me. Or at least, he wants it to be me, and the Council's agreed.'

'At *your* age, lad!' said Dick Reeves. 'How old are you, Adam?'

'Twenty-two.'

'A Reader of twenty-two! Times is changing, aren't they?' Dick sounded doubtful about the idea.

'There's no one more suitable!' Hester pronounced.

'And, Adam,' said Beth softly, 'we'd have a house!'

'That's right,' said Adam. 'We could get married. William says he'd give up his house. He and Sarah'd move in with their old Aunt Ellen, who wants looking after and hasn't long to live anyway.'

'The Reader's house!' Beth's eyes shone. 'The best house in the village, ours! I can't believe it!'

'It's a temptation,' Adam said.

'A temptation?' Beth came swiftly to earth. 'You mean you mightn't take it? Why shouldn't you?'

'Because,' said Adam, 'it's not just a matter of being the chief person. It means learning what's in the Book, and conducting the Prayer Day meeting, and all that sort of stuff!'

'If William Jonas can do it, you can,' said Beth. 'And you're the best person for the job. You got more sense than anyone else on Halcyon. You ain't got any right to turn it down. In fact you got a duty to accept!'

Adam put an arm round Beth.

'It's the house you're after, really!' he said.

Beth smiled in apologetic admission.

'It might be years before we could get enough timber together to build our own,' she said. 'And we aren't getting any younger.'

'No,' said Adam, teasing her. 'You're every day of twenty, aren't you?'

'Well, I'm ready to be married.'

'Oh, Adam, take it!' urged Molly. 'And bring those poor people back from Kingfisher!'

'That's what I want to do,' said Adam. 'But I'd have to carry an Island Meeting with me. With a hard winter coming, it wouldn't be easy.' He pondered. 'It all comes back to the Teaching. If we could get rid of the idea that incomers are sent by the Bad One, it'd all be much easier. And if only Kingfisher wasn't forbidden as the Bad One's territory . . . The trouble is that I can't read, any more than William can. I don't know whether all that stuff about the Deliverer and the Bad One is really according to the Book at all. I've only got William's word for it, and he's only got the word of the Reader before him.'

'We need someone who can read,' said Thomas.

'Do you think it's very difficult, Adam?' Hester asked. 'Could *you* learn?'

'I don't know,' Adam said. 'I never had a chance to try.'

'It can't be all *that* hard,' said Thomas thoughtfully. 'Charlie Herrick can read. He has rows and rows of books, and says he's read them all. I don't think he's cleverer than you are, Adam.'

'What I need is somebody to teach me,' Adam said.

Then the thought came at once to all of them.

'Charlie!'

'Do you think he would?' Adam asked.

'Well,' said Thomas, 'he's fond of those books of his. I think he might *like* teaching someone else.'

'Of course, if he was willing,' said Adam, 'Charlie could read the Book to us now!' He went on, excitedly, 'That's the answer! I shall tell William Jonas I'm only going to be Reader if we can bring Charlie over here and get him to read us the Book!'

'Do you think William will agree to that?' Hester asked.

'Yes, I do. Why shouldn't he? His own position won't depend on it any more. And he's weary. William will agree to anything that lets him retire.'

'But will Charlie Herrick agree?' asked Molly.

'Well, that's another question. He says he likes to be left in peace. He may take a bit of persuading.'

'And who's going to persuade him?'

'You are,' said Adam. 'You're coming over to Kingfisher with me as soon as we get a fair day for sailing.' He grinned. 'You might even see Otipo again.'

Molly blushed.

'Dan Wilde called in here on his way to the fishing,' Hester Reeves told Molly. 'You was out milking Daisy. He hadn't time to wait. He's coming back this evening. He wants to walk out with you.'

'Oh, *does* he?' said Molly, irritated. 'Well, *I* don't want to walk out with *him*!'

'Seems your dad told him he could.'

'My dad don't speak for me. Not when it comes to walking out. Dan'll be asking for me next, and I don't want him.'

'You could do worse than Dan Wilde,' said Beth. 'The Wildes got a good house and a big vegetable plot and a bullock cart and more sheep than anyone else on Halcyon. Jacob Wilde's very respectable, even if it don't look as though he'll be Reader. And Dan's strong and been out at the fishing these two years past. I wouldn't turn up my nose at Dan Wilde if I was you, Molly.'

'It's all very well for you,' grumbled Molly. 'You've got Adam. There ain't no more Adams on Halcyon.'

'Well, *that's* true enough, Molly Reeves,' said Hester. 'In fact there ain't many young men at all, as well you know, since *Petrel* was lost. If you refuse Dan, you mightn't get anyone.'

Molly was sullenly silent.

'Truth is,' Beth told her mother, 'she *still* fancies Otipo.'

To her intense annoyance, Molly felt herself blushing yet again.

'I'll admit, he's real nice,' said Beth. 'Adam thinks well of him, too. But he's not for you, Molly. You'd best put him out of your mind.'

'How can I put him out of my mind?' Molly demanded, enraged. 'Or any of them, stuck there on Kingfisher with winter coming!'

'Adam's doing his best,' Beth said. 'But remember, it's going to be a hard winter for all of us. And in the meantime, Molly Reeves, if I was you I wouldn't be in a hurry to fall out with the Wildes.'

'That's right, Moll,' her mother said. 'Remember that if there's another meeting about the New People we'll want the Wildes to be on our side. And it's not just that. You know there'll be trouble with your dad if you send Dan Wilde packing.'

'Oh, all right,' said Molly, who knew both these things perfectly well but still found that the more she thought about Dan Wilde the less she wanted his attentions. Still, when he came to the house at the end of the day's work, she agreed to walk with him. She didn't argue when he took her down toward the Dell, where the courting couples went, or even when he held her big warm hand in his even bigger one.

Dan's usually bovine face wore an amiable grin.

'You're a grand big lass, Moll,' he told her. 'I allus said you was, even when my mum called you a great lump.'

'Oh, she called me *that*, did she?' said Molly, nettled.

'But I told her straight,' Dan went on. '"I don't mind," I said. "I like a good strong 'un with plenty of work in her. And something to get hold of."'

He put an arm round Molly's waist. Molly wondered whether to object, but decided she shouldn't. They arrived in the small grassy hollow, out of sight of the village, to which they'd been heading. It wasn't private enough for anything very startling to happen, but it gave a little protection from prying eyes.

'Still, even if you *are* strong, you're not as strong as me, are you, Moll?' said Dan. 'Want to wrestle?'

'If you like,' said Molly without enthusiasm. Wrestling was an accepted activity between island boys and girls. It offered you physical contact on a scale that could be varied according to the degree of eagerness or reluctance on either side. Bodies could be pressed together fiercely or gently, experimentally or lovingly or ardently or hardly at all. Wrestling was a language, and Molly didn't intend to say much in it. But Dan forced the pace rather more than she thought he should: not actually trying to reach any improper degree of intimacy, but meeting her resistance with superior smiles and renewed pressure.

A moment came when Molly had a close view of the bristle on his cheeks and chin, and, as he panted with exertion, caught the smell of his breath, which was fishy. It wasn't fair to object to this. Dan wasn't the only islander whose breath ever smelled of fish. But suddenly she felt a physical distaste for him. And although Dan's ox-like strength was indeed greater than hers, he wasn't manoeuvrable or well coordinated. Molly caught him off balance, swiftly exerted all her force, and threw him on his back on the grass.

Dan sat up, shocked and bewildered. For a moment he looked as though he was going to return to the fray and fight her in earnest. Then he grinned and got peaceably to his feet, rubbing his rump.

'Aye, you're a good 'un, Moll,' he told her. 'There's not another lass on Halcyon could do that. Well, just you wait. It'll be different next time. Now, what about a kiss?'

'No,' said Molly.

'All right. It's for you to say. But next time I'll be wrestling you for that kiss, and fighting to win, so watch out!'

Dan was recovering his self-esteem.

'You won't find a better lad than me,' he said, 'and I won't find a better lass than you, so I reckon we're well set.'

'I'm not set for anything,' Molly said.

'We'll see about that,' said Dan. He added admiringly, 'I *said* you're a good 'un, Moll, and I meant it. You are, truly. In my opinion,' he continued with proper emphasis, 'you're good enough for *me*!'

He took her hand, and they walked back toward the village. Molly dreamed all the way that she was with Otipo.

With Adam at the tiller, *Seamew* beached again on Kingfisher. Molly and Thomas were with him, and Wilf Jonas, a younger cousin of the Reader, made up the crew. Abel Oakes hadn't wanted to come. 'I just can't bear it, seeing my two young people and then having to leave them,' he'd said, 'but if you bring Charlie across and he wants a nice quiet place to stay, he can have a berth here in the cave.'

As before, half a dozen of the New People silently surrounded the boat. Mua came forward to meet them. But this time she didn't smile, and her greeting was restrained.

'Adam,' she said. 'Molly. Thomas. I am glad you have come.'

'We've brought some things,' Thomas said. In the boat they had more sheepskins and old woollen clothing, and as much food as they'd been able to scrape together, which wasn't much. There were a couple of sacks of small but precious potatoes, a few other vegetables, some dried fish, and a capful of hen's eggs from Hester Reeves.

Adam and Thomas began to unload this tiny cargo. But then the tall aloof Rikofian called out some words in his own tongue and held up a hand, in an unmistakable gesture to them to stop.

They stared at each other. The Rikofian spoke to them again, and then to Mua.

'What's he saying, Thomas?' Adam asked. But Thomas's grasp of the incomers' language wasn't good enough to cope. He could only shake his head.

'Tamaru says,' Mua told them slowly and with some embarrassment, 'that we should not accept these gifts.'

'But why?' Thomas asked. 'You took them from us before.'

'He says that it should not continue. We receive gifts only from our friends. Those who do not want us on their island are not our friends.'

'But *we* want you!' said Thomas crossly. 'None of *us* had anything to do with rejecting you. Can't you tell him that?'

Mua turned to Tamaru. A dialogue followed, in which two or three of the other Rikofians also took part. At length Tamaru inclined his head in what appeared to be reluctant acceptance.

'I don't know why we bother,' muttered Thomas to Adam as they unloaded the few remaining supplies. 'Not that I expect them to be grateful, exactly, but I wish they'd look just a *bit* pleased when we bring them something.'

'Tamaru is proud,' said Mua with dignity.

'And I reckon you are, too,' Thomas told her. 'Anyway, how are you managing?'

'We live. We do not live well, but we live.'

'Tell them we're still hoping to get them back to Halcyon,' said Adam.

Thomas tried to explain to Mua that Adam was likely to become Reader and would try to get the former decision reversed. Mua translated to her fellow-Rikofians. There was a general discussion among them, in which Tamaru was prominent. Eventually Mua said,

'We would rather stay here than go where many people do not want us.'

'But if everyone on Halcyon *did* want you?' Thomas asked.

'Then it would be different.'

'In the meantime, can you get through the winter?' Adam asked.

'We shall see,' said Mua. 'We shall not die easily. But if we must die, we know how to do so.'

'Don't talk like that!' Thomas said; and then, 'You speak our language much better than you used to.'

'Yes. Sometimes Otipo and I go to see Charlie. He teaches us.'

'Where *is* Otipo?' Molly blurted out.

At last Mua smiled.

'He is with Charlie now.'

'In Charlie's hut?'

'Yes.'

'We may as well go there,' said Adam. 'The sooner we talk to Charlie the better for everybody. But it's a struggle, isn't it? We need to change people's minds, both here and on Halcyon. What do you think will bring them all together, Thomas?'

'I've no idea,' said Thomas helplessly. 'I give up.'

'*I* don't give up,' declared Molly.

'Well, so it's you again!' said Charlie Herrick. 'What have you done with your drunks?'

'Left 'em behind,' said Adam, grinning. 'You won't be troubled with *them* on this trip.'

'What's the trip for, anyway?' asked Charlie.

'We wanted to talk to you.'

'How do you know *I* want to talk to *you*?'

'Oh, *Charlie*!' protested Molly. 'I thought you were my friend!'

'There, there, me dear,' said Charlie. 'I'm sorry. It always takes me aback when faces appears at the door. But come into my hut and see who's here!'

He threw the door open. Molly's heart leaped.

'Otipo!' she cried. And regardless of everyone around her, she embraced him energetically. Otipo seemed a little bewildered, but not at all reluctant. Adam and Thomas grinned. Wilf Jonas looked slightly shocked.

'Best not let Dan Wilde hear about that,' he observed. But Molly didn't care about Dan Wilde. She radiated delight.

'Adam's going to be Reader!' she cried. 'And we'll get you to Halcyon again whatever anyone says, just you see!'

'Not so fast, Molly,' said Adam. 'Let me try to explain.' And while Molly held firmly to Otipo's hand, Adam told of William Jonas's proposal and of his response.

'It seems to me, Charlie,' he said, 'that if I'm to be Reader, it's high time I learned to read!'

'Aye, well, that sounds reasonable,' Charlie said. He took out his pipe and began to fill it from a leather pouch. The islanders, who hadn't seen anyone smoke since the last ship called six years earlier, watched with fascination.

'But I need somebody to teach me,' Adam went on.

'Meaning me?' asked Charlie.

'Well, yes.'

'I dare say I could teach you, if you're not stupid,' Charlie said. 'In fact if you're half as clever as Mua and old Teepo here, you'll soon pick it up. Even so, it ain't something you can learn overnight. How you going to get here for lessons?'

'That's the problem,' Adam admitted. 'I'll have so much to do on Halcyon as Reader that I won't be able to keep crossing to Kingfisher. There's only one way really, Charlie. Couldn't you come over to us?'

'Oh!' said Charlie. 'I thought I told you I like a bit of peace. You call that peace, coming over to a place with a hundred people in it? It'd feel like London or New York, compared with Kingfisher.'

'How can I persuade you, Charlie?' asked Adam.

'I don't know that you *can*,' said Charlie. 'I'm not all that easily persuaded, you know. I get set in my ways.'

'Charlie,' said Molly, 'if we can get all the New People home to Halcyon, there'll only be you living on Kingfisher. Then things'll be just as they used to be, and you'll have your peace and quiet.'

'If,' said Charlie. 'If, if, if. If wishes were horses, beggars would ride, they say.'

'I never seen a horse,' said Molly; and then, recalling her duty and inveigling him shamelessly, 'Come to Halcyon, Charlie. Do it for me!'

'Why, you minx!' said Charlie. 'I'm not took in when you eye me like that. It's old Teepo you fancy, not me!'

'I like you, too, Charlie.'

'But not the same way, eh? Oh, I know how the land lies.' And then, indulgently, 'Well, I might. I've quite enjoyed helping Teepo and Mua. And I don't mind seeing Halcyon, now that I'm so close to it. But I don't want to be there for ever. This is my place now. You promise to bring me back?'

'That's a promise,' said Adam. And then, hesitantly, 'There's another thing we'd like you to do while you're there. We'd like you to read the Book.'

'What book?'

'It was written by the man who founded Halcyon, over a hundred years ago.'

'You might not be able to read it, Charlie,' said Thomas cunningly. 'It's all handwritten.'

Charlie was offended.

'I can read handwriting!' he declared indignantly. 'Leastways, I never failed yet. If it's readable by any soul on earth, you can bet your boots Charlie Herrick will read it!'

'Really, we need everyone on Halcyon to hear it,' Adam said. 'The best thing of all would be if you could read it out in the Meeting-House.'

'A public reading!' said Charlie. 'I ask for peace and quiet, and you offer me a public performance! You think you can make a monkey of old Charlie, don't you? Well, we'll see.'

Molly got the impression that the idea had some appeal for him, all the same.

'Of course, if I *did* come,' he said thoughtfully, 'I'd need to bring a few things with me. Some of my own books, to begin with. And my navigational instruments, for safe keeping. And my little friends.'

'Welcome to Halcyon, Mister Herrick,' said the Reader the following day. 'I'm glad to give you the pleasure of meeting me. You've been a good deal in the Outside World, I hear. Well, I've met folk from the Outside World before, so you might say I'm a man of wide experience, but still, I'm very willing to meet another. And Adam here tells me you're a man of learning, too.'

'I got a few books,' said Charlie.

'None of 'em as big as *our* Book, I dare say,' the Reader remarked. 'Our Book's as long as your arm, and nearly as wide as it's long. We used to have some of them little ordinary books at one time, but we didn't think much of 'em. They was used to keep the fires burning in a hard winter, and nobody ever missed 'em. We couldn't read, Mister Herrick, and didn't think none the worse of ourselves for that.'

The Reader paused, to let this last observation sink in.

'However,' he went on, 'times change, and young Adam says that if he's to be Reader he must learn to read. Though, mind you, I still have some doubts myself. I'm not entirely sure that reading ain't sinful.'

'It can't be sinful to find out the truth about the Teaching,' Adam remarked.

'Aye, that's so. And there's been remarks made by Abel Oakes and others that could be took as casting doubt on the Book. To my mind, it'd be a good thing if it was read out in the Meeting-House, so that everybody on the island could hear. Then there wouldn't be no room for argument.'

'That's just what I was going to suggest!' said Adam, delighted.

'It'll give authority to what I've always told 'em, won't it?' said the Reader. 'And if there *have* been any mistakes in passing the Teaching on, well, I suppose we ought to know about them. Not that I think there'll be any mistake that matters. I got an excellent memory, Adam, and so I'm told had all the Readers before me. Still, I can't expect *you* to have a memory like mine, good lad though you are. Young folk today aren't what they were when I was young. I got to allow for that.'

He turned to Charlie.

'We'll be honoured, Mister Herrick,' he said, 'if you'll give us the benefit of your learning, and read the Book to us next Prayer Day. And on the same day I shall hand over the Readership to young Adam. I don't doubt I made a wise choice when I picked on him. Of all the folk on Halcyon, he's probably the one what comes closest to measuring up to *me*.'

William beamed.

'And he'll be none the worse for being a married man, which is what he's about to become. We got it all worked out. Next Prayer Day's going to be quite an occasion. My retirement, Adam getting married and taking over as Reader, and the Book being read out for all to hear, by a man of learning! It'll be a great day in the history of Halcyon!'

Chapter 11

LUKE Jonas rang the Meeting-House bell loudly and long. Stiff in their Prayer-Day clothes, the islanders assembled. Even the oldest uncles and aunties were there. Everyone knew what was to happen, and nobody wanted to miss it.

Now that he was about to cast off his burden, the Reader looked brisker and less bowed than of late. He stood outside the Meeting-House in a little group with Charlie Herrick and Adam, waiting until all the villagers were inside. Charlie was a sight to be remembered on Halcyon for generations to come. He wore a top hat with curly brim, a peacock-blue cutaway coat, high collar and a big bow tie, primrose-yellow waistcoat and gray striped trousers.

'Belonged to the cap'n,' he told those near him, in a loud whisper. 'I saved 'em from the wreck. Don't fit me too well, and a bit out of date, but they're me best clothes. Never thought I'd get a chance to wear 'em.' And the islanders were little inclined to criticise the fit or to find such splendour old-fashioned. They looked and admired.

'You've read the Book to yourself by now, haven't you, Charlie?' Adam asked him.

'Oh, yes. I spent all yesterday evening on it. It wasn't no problem. I told you, there's not much Charlie Herrick can't read. Most of it's in a good hand; just the last few pages is difficult, as if they was written by somebody that hadn't had much practice lately. But, Adam, don't nobody here know what's *in* that Book?'

'It's supposed to be the Teaching,' Adam said. 'We want to find out if it's the same as the Readers have all said it is.'

'Seems to me it might surprise you,' said Charlie.

'You must read it out, whatever it says,' William Jonas told him. 'All my life I've had faith in the Deliverer, and I shan't start having doubts now. I'm not afraid of the truth. And with a new Readership about to begin, this is a good time for making sure we have the message right.'

'Oh well,' said Charlie. 'I suppose you know what you're about. I'm just doing what I've been asked to do.'

'I think everybody's inside now,' said William. 'Shall we go in?'

There was silence in the Meeting-House, and all eyes were on Charlie as he took up his position between the retiring Reader and the incoming one. For once, William rattled through the service and cut out his address to the people. Then he told the islanders,

'It's a sad day for you all, in one way. I, William Jonas, your Reader since the year the *Electra* called at Halcyon, have decided that now in the evening of my days I must give up the duty and pleasure of leading you.'

Several islanders drew breath sharply. Though it was no surprise, they were still awed by the importance of the announcement.

'Many of you know,' William went on, 'who is to have the difficult task of following in my footsteps. However, before I officially hand over to young Adam here, I have one last pleasant duty, which is that of making him a happy man. Elizabeth Reeves, step forward.'

The Reader then went without stumbling through the words of the marriage ceremony as performed on Halcyon.

'That's one of the many things you'll have to learn, Adam,' he remarked when Adam and Beth had been pronounced man and wife. 'Likewise the naming ceremony for babies, which I don't doubt you'll be needing for your own before too long. And there's the burial service, too. I better teach you that quick, 'cause it looks to me as if old Auntie Ada Wilde could be needing it soon.'

William turned to face the gathering.

'And now,' he said, 'with the approval of the Council of Elders, I shall install your new Reader. Whether young

Adam Goodall will do the job as well as what I've done it, I wouldn't like to say. He has a great deal to live up to, a very great deal. And he has problems. We all know we're in for a hard time this winter, and we all know that some folk who shall be nameless haven't been behaving themselves the way they should, especially Harry Kane and Bob Attwood. Well, all I can say is, I want you to accept young Adam as Reader, and do like he says, just as if it was me. And I wish him every good fortune.'

William took the heavy Book from the lectern and planted it firmly in Adam's arms.

'I proclaim you the new Reader, and Governor of Halcyon,' he declared impressively.

Applause broke out all over the Meeting-House, and lasted for some time. Beth looked with fond pride at Adam, then at Molly standing beside her. Molly kissed Beth. Thomas tried to say something to both of them, but it was drowned by the clapping. Adam, with the Book clutched in his arms, spoke hesitantly for two or three minutes, expressing modest doubt about his own abilities. But his voice strengthened and he sounded more confident when he came to his main announcement.

'More important than all this stuff about *me*,' he said, 'is that this is the day we're going to learn what the Book really says. Of course we all know that William has deep knowledge of it, that he got from the Reader before him, who got it from the Reader before *him*. But things get changed a bit by word of mouth, so now we look forward to hearing the Book as it was written.'

There was another round of applause.

'And here,' Adam said, 'is Mister Charles Herrick, former mate of the sloop *Lydia*, who will read the Book to us. And I may say that Mister Herrick has promised to teach the art of reading to me, and if I can I shall pass it on. And who knows, maybe in my lifetime all the children on Halcyon will know how to read!'

There were awed gasps from the audience at this last prospect. William Jonas looked as if he didn't entirely approve, but remained silent. Charlie Herrick stepped forward. Adam presented him with the Book, and Charlie put it in its usual place on the lectern and solemnly opened it. He put on, carefully, a pair of steel-rimmed spectacles. Before speaking, he looked round the audience, as if to make sure he had their attention. Someone at the back giggled, and was frowned at by Charlie and hushed by people nearby.

'I'm sure he's enjoying himself!' whispered Thomas.

'This Book of yours,' Charlie said. 'I wonder how many of you know that threequarters of it is a narrative. I wonder how many of you know what a narrative *is*.'

He paused and looked around. Nobody spoke.

'A narrative is an account of a series of events,' said Charlie, 'often put down at the time they was happening by somebody that took part in them. And this particular narrative was written years and years ago by somebody called Richard Reeves.'

This caused an immediate sensation.

'But the Deliverer's name was Joseph Kane!' protested William Jonas. 'We all know that!'

'Aye, well,' said Charlie, 'the name of Joseph Kane comes into it all right, as you'll soon hear. But I'm the one that can read, and I'm telling you what the Book says. And what it says to begin with is, "A narrative of the settlement of the island of Halcyon, commenced by me, Richard Reeves, 27th September 1788," and if you want to hear what it says you can all keep quiet and listen to me!'

Whispers were still running round the hall at the mention of the name of Reeves, which was one of the eight island surnames. Molly's and Thomas's father was another Richard Reeves. But the whispering died down, and everyone listened intently as Charlie began.

We left Devonport on October 17, 1783, in the brig *Susannah*, commanded by Captain J. R. V. Fitzwilliam, Royal Navy, myself being Second Mate. The object of the expedition was to extend those surveys of the Southern Oceans which had been carried out by the late illustrious Captain Cook, and to discover whether certain crops might be cultivated in newly-opened territories oversea. We carried a crew of thirty-three, and also a geologist, a botanist, a master-gardener and his apprentice. The voyage was expected to last three years. Besides the usual stores, the captain had on board grain and vegetable seed for sowing, and sheep, pigs and poultry.

After calling at Teneriffe and the Cape Verde Islands, and crossing the Equator, we experienced a month of adverse winds and heavy seas, which caused the gentlemen accompanying the expedition to be much indisposed. The weather having improved somewhat, Christmas was celebrated by many of the crew by becoming exceeding drunk, and James Attwood and Jonathan Wilde each received two dozen lashes by the Captain's orders.

Several hearers gasped or murmured at the mention of more well-known island surnames, but Charlie read on without a stop.

On 18th January, this being summer in southern latitudes, we put in at Rikofia, a small and delightful island, where the beauty of tropical flowers and the glossy green of the foliage were welcome to our eyes after so many days of only sea and sky, and no less welcome was the friendly and artistic character of the inhabitants.

'Rikofia!' Molly exclaimed in a whisper to Thomas. 'That's where the New People come from!'

Here repairs to the hull and rigging were put in hand, the *Susannah* having suffered much damage from the heavy seas. The harbour being small, and the inhabitants few and little accustomed to the type of work required, having themselves no vessels except sailing-canoes, the stay at Rikofia was longer than intended, at which Captain Fitzwilliam was much displeased and anxious to be away. The botanist and geologist however were much taken with the place and in no hurry to leave, which might have been said also of the crew, for the members of the fair sex at Rikofia, though not all natives of that place, were of generally engaging appearance and agreeable disposition, so much so that before long many of the officers and crew, among them myself, had formed attachments which they little wished to end.

'Sin!' observed Sarah Jonas severely. 'Oh, they were in need of a Deliverer! And he came, he came!'

'Wait a moment, ma'am, if you please!' said Charlie. 'Allow me to proceed!'

> The repairs being accomplished, the *Susannah* sailed from Rikofia, but with much grumbling and discontent among those of the men who would have stayed there if they could. When we were five days out, the First Mate came to my cabin late at night, and proposed to me that we should lead the disaffected members of the crew in a mutiny, after which we would seize the ship and sail her back to Rikofia, there to be reunited with the fair ones of our choice.
>
> To this, with many misgivings but with my own dear Tamalia in mind, I assented, and, to cut a long story short, at dawn two days later, having taken possession of the armoury and of all the weapons on board, we surprised the Captain and the sailing-master in their shirts and forced them at bayonet-point into the ship's launch, together with the geologist and botanist, the boatswain, and some dozen of the crew who had refused to join us. We cast them adrift with a twenty-gallon cask of water, some salt beef and biscuit, and what happened to them thereafter I know not, only that I never saw them again.
>
> We sailed the *Susannah* back to Rikofia, being now twenty-one in number, and when we arrived, twelve of these went ashore, saying they were finished with the sea, and these, too, we saw no more. But our leader, Joseph Kane, the First Mate . . .

Instantly a gabble of angry or astonished voices broke out all over the Meeting-House. William Jonas leaped forward and stood face to face with Charlie.

'I'd have you know you're speaking of the Deliverer!' he cried.

Charlie removed his spectacles and looked William in the eye.

'I'm aware of that,' he said.

'And you're making out he was leader of a mutiny?'

'I'm not making out anything,' Charlie said. 'I'm just

telling you what's in this Book, that's all. And I'll be glad if you'll let me get on with it!'

William subsided. Charlie put the spectacles back on his nose and went on.

> . . . Our leader, Joseph Kane, the First Mate, argued that Rikofia was too little removed from the trade routes, and that if the Navy sent a vessel in search of us, we were like to be apprehended there, and doubtless hanged for our pains. Kane said he knew of a remoter island in the southern ocean, a thousand mile from all other land, which as yet had no place in the Admiralty charts, and being unpeopled and far from shipping lanes offered us a safer refuge.
>
> Upon our asking what we were to do about our dear ones on Rikofia, he answered, 'Why, for sure, we will take them with us.' And indeed we found the ladies not unwilling, and Kane, having by our votes been appointed Captain, said he was now empowered in accordance with the custom of the sea to marry us to them, and shortly did so. And so on April 27, 1784, the *Susannah*, having now been renamed *Delivery*, sailed again from Rikofia, heading south. Our company now consisted of Captain Kane; myself, whom he had promoted to be First Mate; Robin Miller, midshipman; Davy Goodall, the ship's carpenter; Wilde, Jonas, Attwood and Campbell, able seamen; and Matthew Oakes, the gardener.

Murmurs broke out again as familiar island surnames were heard. All of these except Miller were still in use on Halcyon. William Jonas interrupted once more, and spoke across Charlie to Adam at the other side of him.

'I don't like the sound of this,' he said. 'Maybe we should break it up for now and get Charlie to tell us the rest in private, so we can decide if it's fit for everyone to hear.'

But Adam dismissed this suggestion.

'You said you weren't afraid of the truth, William,' he pointed out. 'Well, now we're getting it.'

'How do we know we're getting it?' demanded William.

'We'll hear the rest and make up our minds,' Adam said. Go on, Charlie. I'm the Reader now. I give the orders.'

Charlie needed no more encouragement. He'd been rolling out the sentences as if savouring each one of them.

There were also our new wives, and four Rikofian men whom we had persuaded to come with us, promising them that they should each have a share in all that the ship contained. On Kane's orders, so that every man might be provided with a female companion, the Rikofians also had wives on board. Thus we were nine men from the *Delivery*, four Rikofian men, and thirteen women of varied descent, making twenty-six in all, which Kane said was enough to people the island. It was agreed that we should form a republic, of which Kane would be the president.

William Jonas now looked a little less apprehensive.

'Aye, that sounds like the act of a Deliverer,' he said. 'As for the mutiny, I dare say it was the cruelty of this captain that made them do it. When do we come to the Teaching?'

'Not for a while yet,' said Charlie. 'This story ain't over. The best or worst of it's still to come.' And he read on.

After leaving Rikofia we had fine weather and a fair wind, though growing colder, and early in June (this being winter) we sighted on the horizon the cloud-circled Peak of Halcyon Island, and great was our relief, for had we missed it we knew not what landfall we might at last have made, nor after how long a time.

That night we lay to, and the next day began four days of strong southeasterly winds which prevented our nearer approach, and then, being at last able to sail round the island, we could find only one good landing-place, and there we dropped anchor while Jos. Kane and a party went ashore in the ship's cutter. They reported the island to be mainly a volcano, and steeply sloping all round, but to have one stretch of good level land where the inlet was, and to have populations of wild goat and many kinds of birds, some of which were unable to fly, and having no fears allowed themselves to be taken by hand and were good eating.

'That's the Island Fowl, Charlie,' explained William. 'There was plenty of those in my grandpa's day, and I dare say there's still some on Kingfisher. But there's none left on Halcyon now. They've all been et.'

The climate even in winter being temperate, with no

148

human life observable, and the seas around appearing to be rich with fish, it was decided that here we should make our home. While the ship lay at anchor, therefore, we removed from *Delivery* all that could be of use to us, recovering as much timber, metal and canvas as we could, and carrying ashore in the cutter and the jolly-boat all our remaining livestock, stores, guns and powder. All this being achieved, President Kane ordered that the ship be put to the torch, so that none might be tempted to change our decision. Thus did we entrust our future to this remote and desolate isle.

'And here we still are,' said William with satisfaction. 'What about the Teaching, Charlie?'

'I told you, you'll have to wait till I get to it!' said Charlie crossly. 'And there might be some shocks for you before then! Now, just let me go on, will you?' He continued,

There was ample stone at hand, and the gardener Oakes having some knowledge of building, he and the carpenter Goodall directed us in putting up homes for ourselves, the ship providing the timber, and this we did as fast as we were able.

During this time we suffered the loss of the youngest member of our company, the midshipman Robin Miller. We had brought ashore from the ship Captain Fitzwilliam's iron sea-chest, which contained a quantity of gold coin and bullion. Kane declared it prudent that this should be kept in case of future need, for we could not be sure that we would be left forever undisturbed. He proposed that it should be hidden in a place known only to ourselves and not to the Rikofians.

Accordingly, one day when the Rikofians were all at work, he set off with Miller in the jolly-boat for the other side of the island, to seek a place of concealment. Later Kane returned alone over land, saying that a great wave had smashed the boat against the rocks, and that Miller and the chest had both been lost. Afterwards we found what remained of the boat, and the greatly bruised body of our shipmate, but of the chest there was never any trace, nor did we much lament it, for the wealth it contained might as well have been pebbles for all the use it was to ourselves.

'That's right,' said William. 'We've never used coins and suchlike on Halcyon. You can get anything you like with them in the Outside World, I'm told, but they don't count for nothing here.'

Charlie, with a longsuffering air, ignored this latest interruption and read on.

> However, we had little time to mourn the loss of our comrade, for there was much to do. Our homes being built, and the ship's stores having lasted through the winter, spring brought myriads of seabirds to nest, whose eggs we took, and also seals and sea-elephants, which we killed and ate some parts of, though not palatable, and recovered oil from their blubber; and Oakes having now sown our potatoes and other vegetables in land we had cleared, all was going well and we felt we had truly found our paradise and the isle was well named Halcyon.
>
> Yet the Rikofian men were in some discontent, for instead of sharing with them Kane had ordained that they should be employed as labourers under our command, and one of them, Onohito, was ordered a dozen lashes by Kane for insolence.
>
> Later in the summer, the wife of James Attwood died of a decline and Jonathan Wilde's wife fell from a cliff, and they two were without wives, though the other settlers had now established their families and several of the women were with child. Wilde and Attwood said they would not be bachelors for the rest of their lives, and Kane ruled that they might take possession of two of the Rikofians' wives.
>
> One of the Rikofians, being much attached to his wife, resisted this ruling, and Kane ordered that he should be flogged to within an inch of his life, which was done.

At this there were horrified cries from all over the Meeting-House, and William Jonas cried out, 'I don't believe it!' But he made no further attempt to stop Charlie's reading. He sat down heavily on the box reserved for the Reader and buried his face in his hands, but continued to listen intently.

> The other Rikofian thereupon surrendered his wife, and the two women became the unwilling partners of Wilde and Attwood. This, together with poor treatment they received, being much resented by the Rikofians, they made a plan to

destroy us all, looking on us as their oppressors. On a certain day one of them, named Akoro, borrowed a musket from Attwood on pretence of shooting a goat, but instead shot and killed Attwood himself. He then called the other three Rikofians together, and they jointly fell upon Wilde in his own house and killed him. They proceeded to the vegetable plots, where Oakes was at work, and shot him, and Goodall running up to see what had occurred was shot in his turn. Jonas fled to the mountainside and Campbell, by falling in pretence of being shot, was able to preserve his life and join him there.

Kane and I were now attacked by the four Rikofians and were fired on and wounded as we tried to escape, but Kane, when they came to finish him off, declared that he had been on their side all along, and had only mistreated them under pressure from his comrades. This they surprisingly believed, while I, being pleaded for by my wife Tamalia, was likewise pardoned, and we were taken to the house of the deceased Jonathan Wilde at the edge of the village, and well treated.

From nine, our ship's company had now been reduced to four, of whom Kane and I were injured and Jonas and Campbell were in hiding. The Rikofian men were likewise four in number, being Akoro, Onohito, Toluku and Manioko, and being in possession of all the firearms they had the upper hand and might do as they would.

However, a few days later, Onohito quarrelled with the other Rikofians over the disposal of the wives of the dead men, killed Toluku, and fled with a musket to the mountainside, where he joined Jonas and Campbell. This so alarmed the other Rikofians that they sent Kane with a white handkerchief to talk to his fellow-countrymen, which he did, and said that if Jonas and Campbell could disarm and kill Onohito they would be accepted by the rest as friends. This they succeeded in doing, and returned to the village, where they were made welcome. Distrustful of the Rikofians however, Kane decided it would be safest to kill them all. He fell upon Akoro with an axe while he was sleeping, and Campbell and Jonas shot the other two. These deeds were done at the house of Jonathan Wilde, which ill-starred dwelling had now seen the violent deaths of five men.

Charlie paused for a moment, but this time nobody sought

to say anything. The whole gathering seemed to have been stunned into silence.

All the Rikofian men being dead, there remained four mutineers and eleven women, but several of the women, resenting the demise of their menfolk, formed a conspiracy to kill us all in our sleep; but this being discovered, we overcame and forgave them, but Kane ordained that in future any female who misbehaved should be put to death immediately.

There was now peace until the following year, when Campbell, who had worked in a distillery in Scotland, made a mash of parsnip root and, converting a great kettle from the *Delivery* into a still, produced a quantity of ardent spirit. Thereafter he and Jonas were drunk for the greater part of their waking hours, and Jonas, while in a state of intoxication, walked off a cliff top and was dashed to pieces on the rocks below.

Campbell, continuing to distil liquor, grew ever more violent and suffered frequent delusions, in one of which he fired at Kane believing him to be Captain Fitzwilliam returning to arrest him, but missed by a wide margin. At this Kane decided he must be removed, and one evening when the man was in a drunken stupor took the axe with which he had killed Akoro and split Campbell's skull in two.

Thus there are now only two of the *Delivery*'s crew left alive on Halcyon, being Kane and myself, though there is a growing infant population, several children having been born since their fathers' deaths. To this tale of murder and treachery have our high hopes of a new and paradisal life descended. Furthermore, though there are still eleven women to two of us, Kane appears not to desire any of those that are available, but ever casts lustful eyes on my own wife Tamalia, of whom I know he would gain possession if he could. Since the killing of Campbell I have slept ill at nights, and I would it were possible not to sleep at all, for I deeply distrust Joseph Kane and dread the look I sometimes surprise on his face.

There was silence again. After a while Adam asked quietly, 'What happened then, Charlie?'

'That,' said Charlie, 'is the end of the narrative of Richard Reeves. I suppose he became Joseph Kane's final victim. May he rest in peace.'

Chapter 12

WILLIAM Jonas, seated on his box, was shaking.

'I just can't take it in,' he said. 'We all know Joseph Kane as the Deliverer. All my life, and my dad's and grandad's before me, was lived in that faith. Now it sounds like he was a murderer and a mutineer.'

'You ain't heard it all yet,' said Charlie. 'There's another page or two that was written by Kane himself. He wasn't much of a hand at writing, but like I said it takes a lot to beat Charlie Herrick, and I've managed to read it. And you better all listen, because it explains a lot.'

The meeting had broken up into little muttering groups. Adam shouted to everyone to be quiet and settle down again, and Charlie went on.

'The rest of this book is dated more than twenty years later,' he said. 'September the eleventh, 1809, as a matter of fact. This is what it says.

> I write this in the skull-shaped cave to which I have so often in recent years retired to think upon the events of my life and of those I brought to this island.
>
> A few days ago, young Timothy Reeves brought to me this book, which had been found on his mother's death, she having hidden it all the years of her widowhood, for which I cannot blame her, for she had much to suffer.
>
> The account given by Richard Reeves is, to my shame, true, and there were other crimes that he did not know of. I have spent the days since reading his words mostly on my knees. For it is true that our community here began in sin, and never can I forget it.

Ten days after I had put paid to poor Reeves's account, there came to me the first of my visions, in which the Bad One himself appeared before me, dancing and rejoicing that he had made me his instrument and had won so many souls for his infernal regions, and did declare to me that my soul too should be his in the end and should suffer the worst torments of all, for that I was the greatest sinner.

But at last came a vision in which a shining Spirit appeared to me and said that as the one grown man in a community of women and children I might yet redeem myself by leading all of them to the Light, and by this means might yet deliver the souls of my suffering comrades. And on rising I swore that I would bring about on Halcyon the triumph of Good over the Bad One and all his works, and that within my lifetime a Meeting-House should be built wherein the people might pray, and I turned away from sin and began to work on the Teaching, in order that all might be saved. And from that day forth until a few nights ago I had no more visions, and the Bad One troubled me no more.

And I told the women that the children must never know of the evil in which they began. And none on the island save myself could read or write, for the women were unlettered and the children were yet young, and I resolved that they should remain untaught, for of knowledge comes only evil. And I resolved that no seaman or other person from the outside world should be allowed to stay on Halcyon, for they too would bring evil to us. And there was a woman that did steal from the other women, and a child that did inflict grievous harm upon another, and I ordered that they be put on the islet of Kingfisher, and that hereafter Kingfisher should be known as the island of sin, and that sinners and persons from the outside world who could not otherwise be dispatched from our shores should be placed upon it for the rest of their lives and should be for ever shunned, and I ruled that no person from Halcyon should set foot on that island.

And all this I declared to be part of the Teaching. And I ordered that all on Halcyon should live in harmony, and that no man henceforth should lift his hand against his neighbour, nor should covet his neighbour's wife, for all these things had brought only trouble. And I ordered that the grazing and the wild creatures of the island should belong equally to all, and that all should share in the boats and in the fruits of fishi but that each man should be allowed his own piece of land to grow vegetables and to keep his own animals.

And I ordered that in time of hardship each person should support all others. And I ruled that each man should keep his wife and children in order, and should permit no laughing or jesting or any violence, be it only in sport, and that all persons should go to worship on Prayer Day, that they might be exhorted afresh to keep sin and the Bad One at bay. All this and much more I have declared to be the Teaching, and have caused to be learned by rote by a chosen few, so that they may hand it down through the ages to those who come after them. And I have ordained that henceforth I be known and addressed as the Deliverer, not out of pride but in recognition of my duty to lead my people out of evil.

And these twenty years past I have withdrawn on many occasions to meditate alone in this cave, seated on the iron sea-chest with its great and useless wealth in gold coin and bars, and have thought upon the lost life of young Miller, who helped me to bring it here and was silenced for his pains. And bitterly have I lamented my evil-doing.

Now, since poor Reeves's narrative was found, I have prayed and fasted afresh, and yesternight I did have a joyful vision, for I saw eight white albatross, or goneys as we call them, ascend into the sky, and the shining Spirit that I had seen before came to me and said they were the souls of my shipmates, which by my good deeds I had caused to be saved. And the Spirit told me that I must write in the Book of what I had done, and that I must place the Book in the Meeting-House and order that it be honoured as the source of the Teaching, for the wickedness of which it tells could now be read by none on the island but myself, and could bring no others to their eternal doom. And I said to the Spirit that at some future time the Book was like to be read by some person coming to Halcyon, and the Spirit told me that when that should happen it would be a sign that the evil was about to depart from our island and that all could now be known.

So I say to those who may read these words, think upon them, and be in fear and trembling, and do no evil, that the Bad One may be powerless and that Halcyon may continue to be a place of innocence. And that you will pray for the souls of me and of those whom I led into illdoing is the earnest entreaty of

The one-time tool of wickedness and
later Deliverer of Halcyon,

Joseph Kane.

Charlie closed the Book.

'The remaining pages,' he said, 'are blank.'

There was a long silence in the Meeting-House. The
islanders, who had been bursting to express their horror,
astonishment or incredulity at the earlier part of the story,
were now overwhelmed. No one knew what to say. At length
William Jonas spoke, in what had become the quavering
voice of an old man.

'We was all born in sin,' he said. 'This island is steeped in
sin.'

Sarah Jonas was more resilient.

'Maybe the Deliverer was a sinner,' she said sharply, 'but
he was still the Deliverer. He repented his wickedness. The
Teaching still stands, don't it?'

'I reckon it does,' said Jacob Wilde. 'We know more about
him now. We know he wasn't perfect, no more than we are.
But he was inspired to lead us. We can't suddenly turn away
from everything he said.'

'That's right,' said Sarah. 'I believed in him all my life, and
I ain't going to stop following him now, and that's a fact.'

The meeting was beginning once more to break up into
separate conversations. Adam called for order.

'This has given us a lot to think about,' he said. 'I agree
with Jacob that we don't have to reject the Deliverer's teaching out of hand, just because we find he wasn't what we
always thought him to be. But I do think we have to start
considering it on its merits rather than accepting it just
because it comes from the Deliverer. And I'm not all that
impressed by the case he makes for sending incomers to
Kingfisher. I think we should ask ourselves again whether it
isn't time we brought the New People back.'

'We'd have to feed them,' Jacob reminded him. 'Twelve
more to share what we've got would be a hard burden to carry
this winter.'

'We're all familiar with *that* argument,' Adam said. 'Well, I don't intend to push for a decision this minute. The New People say they'd rather die than come back unwanted. I reckon it's up to us to make it clear that we're their friends and we do want them.'

'Friends?' Bob Attwood burst out. 'Them savages our *friends?*'

Thomas couldn't restrain himself. He and Molly had only been allowed into the Meeting-House because their sister's wedding was part of the proceedings; otherwise, being officially children, they had no right to be there. But this was too much.

'They're not just our friends!' he shouted at the top of his voice. 'They're our relatives, aren't they? Half the founders of Halcyon were Rikofians!'

'That don't signify!' Bob declared. 'It was years and years ago, and our folk were the bosses and gave the island all its surnames. The savages don't even speak a civilized language!'

'That'll do, Bob!' said Adam; and then, as the meeting grew noisy again, 'Quiet, please! Listen to me! I propose that we should meet here again next Prayer Day. That'll give us a chance to talk things over. Now we must all go home and ask ourselves how this new knowledge will affect our future and the way we live. And we'll decide on Prayer Day what we're going to do about the New People. I declare this meeting closed!'

Molly and Thomas moved toward the Meeting-House door with the rest of the gathering, leaving Beth to wait for Adam. Just ahead of them were Harry Kane and Bob Attwood. The two men stopped outside the Meeting-House door to talk to each other and to Alec Campbell.

Harry looked excited.

'It was my great-great-granpa that did all that!' he said. 'He was quite a feller, wasn't he? He done 'em all in, and got his own way!'

'Away with you, Harry!' said Alec Campbell. 'You won't do all of *us* in, I can tell you!'

'Course not,' said Harry. 'I'm not hankering after *that*. But still, it makes you think. And you know what my Jemmy told me?'

Sensing that he was overheard, he dropped his voice, but continued to whisper eagerly to his friends. Thomas looked at them sideways with suspicion.

'I don't like that,' he said to Molly as they walked home. 'Maybe we were better off ignorant after all. This could put some awful ideas into people's heads.'

'Well,' said Molly, 'the Deliverer said that some time the Book would be read by a person coming to Halcyon, and that would be a sign that the evil was leaving us. Let's hope he was right.'

'The evil leaving us,' said Thomas. 'I wonder.'

Dick Reeves had killed a sheep to celebrate his daughter's wedding, and there was a feast that night in the Reeveses' house at which all the Reeveses and Goodalls and their families were present. This would normally have been a time of good cheer, with bellies filled, tales told, songs sung, and older people passing on reminiscences of their youth, enjoying the chance to talk. But on this occasion the atmosphere was heavy: partly because everyone was in fear of the hard winter ahead, partly because the islanders were still dazed by the contents of the Book, which upturned everything they had ever heard about the origins of their community.

William Jonas, who should have been a guest, had announced at the last minute that he wasn't coming; he had too much to think about. Charlie Herrick wasn't at the celebration either. He'd gone to stay in Abel's cave, the old man's way of life being the nearest he could find to his own; and although he'd promised to give a brief course in reading to a class consisting of Adam, Beth, Molly, Thomas and Abby Jonas, he'd made it clear that he wasn't interested in further socializing.

Molly was furious because her father had invited Dan

Wilde to the party; and Dan sat beside her like an accepted lover and tried to put his arm round her.

'Your Beth's wed,' he remarked. 'Why not you next?' But Molly disdained to reply.

Later, in accordance with tradition, the guests escorted Adam and Beth to their new home, and made a few jokes and suggestive remarks about the married state. The escort then returned from the Reader's house to the Reeveses', where celebrations should have continued into the night. But somehow there was a lack of vitality in the proceedings, and around the usual island bedtime the party began to break up.

For the first time in her life, Molly slept in a bed by herself, without Beth. She found it disturbing, and woke up several times, disconcerted by the absence of the familiar warm body. It felt like the end of an era. And Beth wasn't all that much older than she was. Maybe it was time she was married. Her father would be glad if she accepted Dan. But the thought of embracing ox-like, self-satisfied Dan seemed no more attractive than it had been before.

Next morning was wet, and for three days the rain crashed down. The boats couldn't go out, and no work could be done out of doors. Women as always had plenty to do. Men finished off any odd jobs they could find; then, bored, sat around and groused. Adam was busy, however, going round the houses and discussing with everybody what should be done about the New People. He took Thomas with him on most of these visits. Not being yet accepted as a man, Thomas should not, according to island custom, have had any part in discussing anything; but Adam's newly found prestige as Reader was enough to carry him along.

There was still some reluctance to accept the incomers. Accustomed all their lives to revering the Deliverer, many islanders simply could not bring themselves to disregard his pronouncements. Others agreed with Jacob that the winter would be hard enough without adding to the island's problems; others again felt that by sending the incomers to Kingfisher they had disposed of the matter, and they didn't want to reopen it. Adam argued patiently against all these points of view. By the third day, he and Thomas decided that they probably had a majority. But increasingly they got the impression that others were also moving around the village and seeking support.

The others of course were Harry and Bob. But they seemed to have been selective in choosing houses at which to call. Some people who were opposed to the return of the New People had seen nothing of them. Others had seen them, but wouldn't tell Adam what had been said. There was a good deal of shiftiness and subdued tension. Len Wilde, who'd been sharply warned by the former Reader against any further association with Bob and Harry, declared that he hadn't spoken to either of them, though Thomas was sure he'd seen them both leaving Len's home the previous night. And when Adam and Thomas arrived at Alec Campbell's house to find Bob and Harry already there, the latter two just grinned at them and promptly took themselves off.

The night before the meeting at which the decision was to be made, the sky cleared and the moon came out. Adam and Beth had supper with the Reeveses. Just after supper, Len Wilde came to the door and called to Adam that goats had got into the vegetable plots.

'You're paying the price of being Reader, Adam,' said Hester Reeves, smiling, as Adam hastily dragged his coat on and set off with Len to investigate. Thomas went along to help them. They were away for some time. Beth and Molly, going out to see if there was any sign of their return, noticed more activity than usual going on in the village. Several people moved back and forth between houses; two men whose faces they couldn't see in the dark and at a distance came down the path that led from the headland and Abel's cave, carrying something heavy between them.

Adam returned, tired and cross, to say that some fool had left a gate open and just about every animal on the island had managed to find it. He also complained of the absence of the younger men when there was a job to be done. When Molly remarked on the unusual amount of movement in the village, he groaned.

'I'm sure Bob and Harry are up to something,' he said. 'We'll have to keep an eye on them. There's no peace and quiet on Halcyon these days. Why did I ever let myself be Reader? It's almost enough to make you believe in the Bad One!'

'There, there,' said Beth in a wifely tone. 'Come home to bed!'

Next morning the sun shone and the breeze was light. It looked a perfect sailing day.

'If the vote goes through, we'll be on our way to Kingfisher soon,' Adam said to Thomas outside the Meeting-House. 'And let's hope it's a clear decision by a good majority. I'll be relieved when I've got the New People safely here; I'm not convinced they can survive otherwise.'

Luke Jonas rang the bell, and islanders began to flock to the Meeting-House. But soon it was obvious that something was wrong.

Lazy Lucy Attwood was the first to give voice.

'Where is he?' she demanded. 'Where's me husband?'

'And mine?' wailed Maggie Campbell. 'And me spare blanket, and me taters, and me dried fish?'

'And our Len?' added middle-aged Mary Wilde, Len's mother. 'Where's our lad?'

It soon became clear that at least ten of the younger men — most of the able-bodied men on the island, for the loss of *Petrel* four years earlier had taken its toll — were missing.

'Never mind the meeting for now!' ordered Adam. 'Get down to the landing-place!'

Most of the islanders hurried off toward the landing-place. Some women whose menfolk were missing went back to their own homes to see what else had disappeared. Adam, grim-faced, returned to his own house and took from a hook the clumsy key to the little stone building that served as the island's armoury. He also picked up the telescope he had inherited as Reader, and handed it to Thomas.

'You and Molly go up to the Lookout!' he said.

It wasn't long before an advance guard was hurrying back to the village from the landing-place. All tried to shout at once as soon as they were within earshot:

'Both boats have gone!'

There was dismay on every face. Halcyon depended on the boats for a large part of its livelihood.

Adam didn't need to try the door to the arms store. It was obvious that it had been forced. The guns were gone; so were the long lances used in season for sealing; so was all the powder and shot.

The women whose husbands or sons had disappeared were the most desperate. Not only men, boats, guns and ammunition had gone, but also clothing, bedding, vessels for holding water, and every kind of food that could be carried. Even some chickens had vanished.

Adam led a group of people up toward the Lookout, where Thomas and Molly had both had time to survey the horizon. Thomas passed the telescope over to him.

'There they are!' he said. 'Just to the right of the Point, almost out of sight.'

The boats could just be seen: a couple of specks on the horizon. Not the western horizon, toward Kingfisher, but the eastward one, beyond which lay nothing but a near-infinitude of ocean.

A dozen people all wanted to look through the telescope. Adam handed it to the man next to him.

'No hurry now!' he said ruefully. 'We can't do anything about that!' And then, to Thomas. 'They're heading for the mainland!'

'The mainland!' Thomas could hardly take it in. 'But it's . . . how far?'

'Twelve hundred miles to the nearest port.'

Thomas couldn't visualize twelve hundred miles.

'How long will it take them?'

'Can't tell. Twenty days, maybe, if they're lucky. It all depends on wind and weather.'

'You think they'll make it, Adam?'

'I don't see why not. They've a pair of seagoing boats.'

'*Our* boats!' groaned Jacob Wilde.

'That's the worst part of it!' Adam said. 'We can do without Bob and Harry, but to lose so many men and both our boats! That's a dreadful blow! And *Shearwater*'s a fine boat!'

'*Seamew*'s not as good,' said Jacob. 'She's been neglected since Harry had charge of her. I'm not so sure that I'd fancy an ocean voyage in her.'

'Anyway,' Thomas asked, 'do they know how to set a course?'

And then everyone exclaimed at once,

'Charlie!'

'*He* can navigate!' said Adam. 'Come on! Let's see if he's gone, too!'

He led the way at a loping trot toward Abel's cave. Most of the islanders who were with him soon fell behind, for the remaining men were past middle age and the women were impeded by their heavy skirts. But Thomas kept close behind him, and Molly, when she had outdistanced the others, slipped shamelessly out of her skirt, slung it across her arm, and ran on in her petticoat. Across the upland they ran, past the ill-starred home of Jonathan Wilde where five men had died all those years ago, and along the cliff top. Then there was the scramble across three gulches and the run down the dry bed of the fourth.

'Abel!' shouted Adam as soon as the cave was in earshot. 'Abel!' And Thomas added his voice: 'Abel! Charlie!'

Their voices echoed from the walls of the gulch.

'Abel! Charlie! Abel!'

No reply.

Molly, following them along, had a sudden presentiment of disaster.

'Abel!' she called in turn. 'Abel! Charlie!'

There was still no reply; only a scatter of echoes. They hurried across the sand to the entrance of the skull-shaped cave: the cave where Joseph Kane had come to meditate upon his sins; Abel's cave.

The old man lay sprawled on the ground, unconscious.

Blood from a head wound was matted in his scanty hair and had oozed on to the sand. Of Charlie Herrick there was no sign.

The cave was in disorder, with Abel's possessions flung in all directions. Five or six gold coins were scattered on the floor of the inner cave; Charlie's books were thrown around, too, but his navigational instruments were missing. The pair of cages in which he'd kept his rats lay on their sides, open.

Hours later, in the care of Hester Reeves, Abel became briefly conscious.

'It was Bob,' he mumbled. 'Bob struck the blow. But Harry egged him on. I reckon Harry done this as much as anyone alive. And they took Joseph Kane's chest. I might have known that ill would come of it in the end.'

Molly was on her knees beside him.

'And Charlie?' she asked. 'What about Charlie?'

'Charlie?' The old man repeated the word, looked vacant for a moment, then replied in a barely audible voice, 'Charlie. Yes. They took him off with them. They forced him. He didn't want to go. And they let his rats out.' Then Abel seemed to forget about Bob and Harry and Charlie, and made a few wandering remarks about his Jess and his children. But he came back to Charlie in the end.

'Charlie said,' he began, hesitated, lost the thread and picked it up again. 'Charlie said to watch out for his little friends.'

Abel died in the night without having spoken again. Next day Adam, with a little prompting from William Jonas, conducted burial rites for the first time. Abel's body was laid in the windy burial-ground on the hillside near the Lookout, where generations of islanders had preceded him.

Later that day, Adam borrowed the Wildes' dog Match, and walked back to the cave with Molly and Thomas. Match showed some excitement, sniffed around with interest, and followed two or three trails in the neighbourhood of the cave and up the gulch. But he lost them all. Adam, Molly and Thomas also hunted over the area, looking for some trace of Charlie's little friends. There was none.

'I expect we've seen the last of them,' said Thomas.

'I hope so,' said Adam.

When they were back in the village, he took the other two to Harry Kane's filthy cottage. They found Jemmy cowering in a corner and weeping bitterly.

'Yes, I told my dad about the chest,' he admitted through sobs. 'Him and Bob went to fetch it. They said we'd all be sailing for the outside world, and we'd be rich and have everything we ever wanted for the rest of our lives. But I never saw them again.'

The sobs grew louder.

'My dad left me!' he wailed. 'It was me who told him, and then after that he went off and left me!'

'Poor Jemmy,' said Molly, surprising herself.

'I should save your sympathy, Moll,' Thomas advised her. 'There'll be plenty of calls on it this winter.'

'I haven't cried for Abel yet,' said Molly.

'You will,' Thomas said quietly.

'Anyway, what's to become of Jemmy?' Molly asked. 'Now his dad's gone, he hasn't any relatives here. Nobody'll want him.'

'Beth and I talked about that this morning,' Adam said. 'We're going to take him in.'

'You must be daft,' said Thomas.

'Maybe. But I reckon we can make something of Jemmy. There's a bright, brave lad somewhere inside him. He needs a bit of love, that's all. As for the New People, I don't suppose there'll be any opposition to them now. Considering the way they were treated here in Joseph Kane's day, we owe them equal shares at least in what we have. But I'm afraid it isn't much. And without the boats we've no way of getting across to Kingfisher and fetching them!'

Fourth Wave

*T*HE *hungry winter pounces early on Halcyon. Hardly has the wretchedly poor potato crop been lifted and the plots dug over when the first of the easterly gales screams in to the attack. For six days and nights it batters the island. Seas are mountainous and visibility almost nothing. The little fleet of cottages, their gable ends lying like bows to the wind, ride out the storm, though at night the driftwood roof-timbers groan as if still in ships at sea.*

No one goes near the cliff edges. Part of the path to Abel's cave falls into the sea. Islanders who venture out to see to their longsuffering stock, or to weight their roofs with heavy boulders, are buffeted by sudden bursts of wind, slashed by merciless rain, or at the least drenched in icy spray. Sometimes it seems that only one more gust is needed to blow human life off Halcyon for ever.

Yet the seventh day dawns golden. The sky is a perfect rainwashed blue, the sea calmly reflective, the Peak serene in its soft white halo, the outline of Kingfisher clear on the horizon. For a while the weather has suspended hostilities and shows a face of deceptive innocence. But islanders know better than to trust it. It will be villainous again before long.

Chapter 13

ADAM took Dick Reeves and Thomas through morning sunshine to a conference at Jacob Wilde's house. Adam, Dick and Jacob were the only fully-grown active men left on Halcyon; all other males were either young or old.

'It seems to me,' Adam said, 'that from now on the boys will have to be men. And the girls too, so to speak. We can't afford to have them staying home and helping their mothers. Molly Reeves and Ellen Oakes and Abby Jonas can dig and climb and herd sheep as well as anyone else. Or if they can't, they'll have to learn.'

'Molly can,' said Thomas. 'Just give her the chance.'

They went round the village and made a quick tally of food reserves. The results were discouraging. The deserters had taken everything they could lay their hands on. There were barely enough potatoes to keep for seed. Other vegetables were less scarce, and there were still some apples from the scruffy trees in the Dell, but this was nothing like enough to keep ninety souls alive for a winter.

'We'll have to kill all the animals except a few for breeding,' Adam said. 'That means future shortage, but we can't help it. Even then, there won't be enough.'

'We better kill the dogs, too,' said Jacob. 'We can't afford to keep them fed. People can herd sheep without dogs.'

'I'm not so sure about the dogs,' Adam said. 'We might be glad of them. I keep thinking about those rats of Charlie's.'

'Oh, *those!*' said Jacob. 'There was only a few of them, wasn't there? They're probably dead by now.'

'I hope so,' said Adam. 'But if you don't mind, Jacob, we won't kill the dogs while ever we can avoid it.'

'Oh, well, you're the Reader,' said Jacob. He seemed relieved that in this crisis the Readership wasn't his responsibility. 'But you know what we got to do as soon as we can?'

'Yes,' said Adam. 'Build a new boat.'

'That's right. And it won't be easy. It hasn't been done in years. We've not had the wood.'

'Have *you* ever built a boat, Jacob?' Adam asked.

'I've helped. But it was a while ago. Old Ben Attwood and William Jonas are the ones who know.'

'Right,' said Adam. 'We'll put them in charge. We'll take the timber from Harry Kane's house. And from Bob Attwood's, too, if we need it.'

Lazy Lucy Attwood and Maggie Campbell, whose husbands were among the deserters, had moved in together and set up a quarrelsome joint household, uniting only to repel anyone who tried to keep the peace between them. Bob's house, as well as Harry's, was empty. Both could be used as sources of timber.

The old men of the village were ready enough to set about building a boat. 'But it'll take time, young Adam,' said Uncle Ben Attwood. 'There's no hurrying a boat. Not if you want to stay alive in it, in the seas we have here.'

'Quick as you can, Ben, please,' said Adam. 'Or we won't be staying alive anyway.'

There were many days when it wasn't fit to work out of doors. But down at the landing-place a rough-and-ready boat began to take shape. The ribs were made of apple-tree wood from the Dell; 'you can't use driftwood for *them*,' said Ben decisively. Over these, long horizontal members were laid. The timber had to be hewn and sawn with rusty old tools, then pieced and patched together. And then the frame had to be left outside to weather and set in the shape into which it had been lashed. The last stage would be to nail on a covering of sail canvas, thickly smeared with sheep's tallow.

Adam shook his head from time to time over the skeleton as it lay like that of some battered monster on the beach.

'This boat's old before it's even new,' he remarked to

Thomas as time went by and the days grew shorter.

Meanwhile Halcyon survived on a scanty diet of vegetables, with the addition of a taste of meat from the weekly killing of two or three of the island's precious sheep. Without boats there was no fish. There was a little milk, but that was for the youngest children. Cathy Oakes gave birth to her baby by Harry Kane: a thin, undersized child which she doggedly suckled.

Like Jacob Wilde, the remaining members of the old Council of Elders were glad to leave matters in Adam's hands. 'We got a new young Reader,' said Uncle Ben, summing it up, 'and I reckon we should trust him.' Adam set up a new informal council, consisting of himself, Dick and Hester Reeves, and Jacob and Rebecca Wilde. Molly and Thomas didn't belong to it, but they saw its members daily and felt closer than they'd been before to the centre of things.

Adam continued to hold the Prayer Day meetings. Coming together to sing the old hymns cheered and united the islanders; and Adam concluded with a brief prayer to whatever Power might be to help the people help themselves. At each meeting he asked for suggestions for getting Halcyon through the winter; and the first of these came from Abby Jonas.

'Why don't we light a bonfire at the Lookout?' she asked. 'As a distress signal. A ship might come by and see it.'

'That's a good idea, Abby,' said Adam. 'But how would we keep it fuelled?'

'We can take gangs of children out gathering island oak,' said Molly. 'It burns even when it's green. Makes a lot of smoke, though.'

'Well, that's all right,' Adam said. 'Smoke rises. It'll be visible from miles away. Yes, let's light a fire whenever it's fine enough and we've got fuel.' And day by day islanders who had no other task led parties of children on long scrambles round the far parts of Halcyon, where the twisted and scrubby island oak still grew in profusion. But it took a lot of work to keep the bonfire going; and as days went by and no ship came, enthusiasm dwindled.

Adam himself put forward the next suggestion. He had hesitated a long time before doing so.

'There's albatross that winter up on the Peak,' he said. 'Goneys. They nest in the crater hollow and feed the chicks till spring. A party of climbers could get up there and take some. Goney chicks are good eating.'

There was a dazed silence in the Meeting-House. To kill the wandering albatross was to flout the tradition of centuries. After a pause William Jonas declared darkly, 'There's souls of drowned sailors in them birds. And a curse on all that take them.'

'And *murdered* sailors,' added Sarah. 'Remember what the Deliverer said? He saw the souls of his shipmates rise to the sky in the form of goneys.'

'I shouldn't think those particular souls are still around,' said Adam.

'Well, I don't like it!' William retorted. 'I wouldn't have had it in my day as Reader!'

'I don't like it either,' Adam admitted. 'It's a dangerous climb, and these are the last goneys left on Halcyon. I don't want to drive them away. But when folk are hungry . . .'

'Drop it, Adam,' advised Dick Reeves. 'You're upsetting everyone.'

The feeling of the meeting was clearly against the idea. Adam dropped it for the time being, but took up a suggestion from old Auntie May Goodall, who recommended eating one of the local seaweeds.

'We was reduced to it one year when I was a little 'un, eighty years ago,' she said. 'We called it famine weed. I can't say I'd eat it for choice, but it's better than nothing.'

Helped by a couple of younger people, she hobbled down to the shore and showed the islanders how to identify the weed. Boiled in pots over the fire, it put some bulk into the diet and calmed the unease of empty bellies. But it was tough and unpalatable, and didn't seem to give much nourishment. As the days passed, adults grew thin and lethargic, children deceptively pot-bellied. The old men lost interest in boatbuilding and spent most of their time sitting vacantly at home.

'Sometimes I feel like giving up myself,' Adam admitted to Molly and Thomas. 'If we don't act soon, we're lost.' At the next Prayer Day, when fewer than half the remaining islanders had the energy to come to the Meeting, Adam revived the project of scaling the Peak in search of albatross. This time it was greeted with general apathy. William and Sarah Jonas, for the first time in many years, hadn't managed to get to the Meeting-House; they were said to be feeble and depressed. No voice was raised in challenge. With many misgivings, Adam went ahead.

In the end the climbing party consisted of Adam, Molly and Dan. Jacob was left out because the climb was thought to be too hard for a man of fifty, Dick because he couldn't overcome his belief that no good would come of it, and Thomas because Adam knew he hated climbing and took care to find another duty for him.

They set off before dawn on a fine day, crossing the upland plateau, two small gulches and the cranberry bog before scrambling into Big Gulch and heading up it for a couple of miles toward the centre of the island. From the head of the gulch there was a further long climb over a steepening, sparsely-grassed slope. Looking round and down, Molly could see the grey-green plateau far below, fringed with a white lace of surf. The stone of the islanders' homes and vegetable plots was hardly distinguishable from their surroundings; it didn't look from here as if humanity had made much impression on the bare, bleak land.

They trudged upward, through the damp clinging shroud of cloud that circled the Peak. Above, the sky was clear, and sunlight lit the clouds like snowy fields. The last stage of the steepening ascent was over loose scree and volcanic rubble, with showers of pebbles dislodged at every step and only a few jagged handholds to save them from slipping back at each attempt. Weeks of poor diet had weakened Molly more than she realized, and by the time they arrived at the crater she was exhausted.

Here all was grey, sterile and ominous-looking. Molly shuddered, and more than half believed there was a curse at work. But Adam had not been mistaken. The shallow, saucer-like crater hollow was white with albatross. Woolly-downed young birds, fat as butter, sat on scraped-up earthy nests while the old ones, unafraid of enemies, stalked around them.

Adam and Dan moved in. Adam protected Dan with a big stick against the parent birds, which made a great fuss and noise, while the young ones clacked their beaks loudly until Dan silenced them. Molly turned away, not wanting to see the execution. Her role was only that of porter.

In twenty minutes the sacks they'd brought were filled with the bodies of young albatross. Before they began the descent, Adam addressed the seething mass of deprived parents.

'I'm sorry,' he said. 'It was you or us. Come back next year.'

The burdened climb down, over steep slopes of loose rubble, was a nightmare even to surefooted Molly. Once she took hold of a bit of projecting rock, only to feel it break off in her hand. As she grabbed at another handhold, the useless one slid hundreds of feet down the mountain-face. At another point Dan was stuck; Adam and Molly converged upon him and, after a moment when it seemed that all three would fall, they got him moving again.

It seemed an endless time before there was firm ground underfoot. Then weariness took over from fear, and Molly was hardly aware of plodding down Big Gulch, across the cranberry bog and home. Most of the villagers who were fit to do so had turned out to meet them.

'You see?' Adam said. 'So much for the curse.'

'There's time for it to work,' said Dick Reeves gloomily.

'We'll all have a proper meal tonight,' Adam went on. 'It's no good trying to spin this bit of food out. We need to get some strength back.'

The islanders fed well that night on young albatross, fried in its own fat. For many it was a guilty feast, but for once they went to bed with the comfort of full bellies.

They were hungry again next day. And they had let the bonfire go out.

Once more it was Molly who saw the sail first. She was on top of Sammy's Cliff, looking for wild celery in the long wet grass and scanning the sea from time to time, as the islanders all did more and more, in the hope of seeing a ship.

The sail was tiny at first, and brown, and not much more than a dot on the curved horizon. It was coming in fast on the wind, and standing up from the sea's dark sullen surface. Memory of a similar sight, months earlier, stirred in Molly. In a minute she was sure, and was hurrying down to the village and onward to the landing-place, calling to other villagers as she went.

It was the canoe with the outrigger, and it ran in sweetly through the opening in the reef and then between the rocks. There were three people on board. Two of them leaped out and held the boat against the backwash. They were Otipo and the tall, muscular Tamaru. Most of the islanders stood around, lacking energy to help them; but Dan Wilde and Adam were there, and the canoe was dragged up on to the black sand. Out of it stepped Mua. She was taller than when formerly seen on Halcyon, and more dignified; but she moved swiftly to embrace Molly, and then addressed Adam.

'We saw the smoke of your fire,' she said. 'We wondered for many days what we should do. Then we thought that perhaps you had trouble and we should come.'

'We *do* have trouble,' said Adam. 'We lost our boats and most of our men. We're only just surviving.'

Mua looked at the weary faces around her.

'I think you are worse off than we are,' she said. 'We shall give you what help we can.'

Chapter 14

'WE are all in good health,' Otipo said later. 'We have the canoe, so we can fish. We have killed a few of the goats, but there are plenty left. We have found seabirds that stay on Kingfisher in winter, and have taken them for food. But there are so few of us, and we lack company. Where is my friend Charlie?'

He and Mua wept without embarrassment when they heard what had happened to Charlie and Abel. They offered sympathy, but tactfully refrained from indignation, when told how Harry and the other men had deserted. And after discussion with Tamaru and with Adam's new council, they readily agreed to join forces with the Halcyon islanders.

'We can all do as well here as on Kingfisher,' Otipo said. 'I think Kingfisher is better to visit occasionally than to live.'

Tamaru had difficulty in following what was said, but smiled and shook hands all round when it became clear that everybody was in agreement.

'I thought at first he didn't like us,' Thomas remarked. 'And I can't say I'd blame him.'

'He didn't like it when we were locked up,' said Otipo. 'Or when we were taken to Kingfisher by men with guns. He was hurt in his pride. But Mua and I have told him that you and Adam are our friends. And our friends will be his friends, because he and Mua are . . .'

He paused, lost for a word.

'Are to be married?' Molly asked, jumping to a conclusion.

'Yes. They are to be married. It would have been so on Rikofia also, when Mua reached the proper age. She is content. She likes him.'

'So there's no question of you and Mua . . .?'

Otipo smiled.

'No, no,' he said. 'Mua and I are as we have always been. We are like brother and sister. I have other hopes.'

The remaining Rikofians were ferried over from Kingfisher two or three days later. They brought with them goat-meat, and seabirds they had caught, and vegetables from Charlie Herrick's garden.

And it was soon clear that the reappearance of the incomers was a turning-point for Halcyon. The Rikofians were swift of hand and eye, and better than the islanders at all kinds of hunting and fishing. On two successive days they went out in the canoe and caught bluefish and snoek enough to feed the combined populations. They put new life into the flagging construction of the new boat. Eventually it was launched, and though it creaked ominously and wasn't by any means water-tight, it was considered safe enough for fair-weather fishing. On land, the Halcyon ways of cultivation were strange to Rikofians, but they cheerfully learned to double-dig, and helped to turn over a bigger area for the next year's vegetables. The air of disaster which had hung over Halcyon began to lighten.

Adam agreed with Mua that instead of being separately accommodated the Rikofians should be divided among island households. This proved to be a brilliant stroke. Any traces of distrust on either side were soon dissolved in the knowledge of a shared plight. On the long winter nights, and the wet or galetorn days when no one could get outside, Rikofians and islanders spent long hours trying to learn each other's languages and delighting in such comprehension as they could achieve. Old people among the islanders recognized a few almost-forgotten Rikofian words and phrases that had been used on Halcyon in their youth and had obviously come from Rikofian ancestors.

A Rikofian girl, Aola, small and pretty and younger than Molly, came to share bed and board with her at the Reeveses'.

Aolo wept a little at first, but soon began to see herself as a member of the family, and awakened fatherly feelings in Dick, who rather enjoyed having a dainty new daughter. Molly was not dainty.

Thomas had an occupation of his own that winter. Soon after Abel's death, he gathered Charlie Herrick's books from the floor of the deserted cave and carried them home. Night after night he pored over them. He'd seen Charlie running a finger along the lines as he read; he'd recognized Charlie's name on flyleaves, and Charlie had shown him how to write his own name, THOMAS REEVES. He remembered in detail a story read out to him by Charlie the night before the public reading of the Book, and could identify the volume it came from. These were all the clues he had to the decipherment of the rows of strange black marks; but he brought all his mental powers to the task, and in the end, though there was much he couldn't understand and much that was simply beyond his knowledge of the world, Thomas could read.

He passed on a little of this skill to Adam, Beth and Molly, but they always had other jobs to do. Surprisingly, the person who came to share his passion for reading was Abby Jonas, the granddaughter of the former Reader. Abby was changing rapidly from a coy, winsome child to a bright, sensible young woman. She and Thomas rubbed minds together, teasing and joking and arguing, and enjoying the play of intelligence in a way that left most Halcyon folk bewildered.

Dan Wilde came repeatedly during the winter to sit at the Reeveses' fireside. He had been a bit resentful at first that Harry Kane and Bob Attwood hadn't even asked him to join them. But the killing of Abel, and the detestation felt by the remaining islanders for those who had deserted them, changed Dan's mind. He was now rather proud of not having been approached.

'They knew I wouldn't have aught to do with that sort of thing,' he said on one occasion. 'My dad and me, we ain't thieves and murderers. We stay where we're needed, and work.'

This was true, and Molly respected him for it. More and more often, when Dan put an arm round her or took her hand in his hefty paw, she made no resistance. When they were by themselves, he frequently kissed her. She never returned his kisses, but Dan seemed quite satisfied and didn't expect any show of affection from her.

Molly didn't often see Otipo alone. When she did, she felt a tremor of physical excitement, and thought there were signs in his face that her interest was returned. She often wondered what he had meant by his remark about his hopes. But they were both a little embarrassed, here on Halcyon. She couldn't now have embraced him as she had done on Kingfisher.

By the end of winter, three old Halcyon people had died and several other islanders were still weak or listless; everyone was thin. But in the early spring the seabirds returned to lay their eggs, and the cliffs were raucous with their noise. The younger islanders and the Rikofians had strength enough to plunder the ledges. Suddenly there was food and to spare, for the eggs could not be kept. With the arrival of spring, too, there were more days when the canoe and the rickety new boat, called *Fulmar*, could go out and fish. And it was time for sowing.

Molly, in rough sheepskin breeches, dug the soil, collected eggs and went out fishing with the men. As spring advanced, she felt stronger than ever, and full of vitality. With Adam, Dan and Thomas she crossed to Kingfisher for five days, during which they dug over and replanted Charlie Herrick's garden. Lifting Day came; the early potato crop was good, and the succeeding weeks went by without blight or bad weather to threaten the main crop.

Many of the older residents decided that Harry Kane and Bob Attwood were no great loss to the community; it was 'good riddance to bad rubbish' as Auntie May Goodall remarked. Jemmy's behaviour was agreed by all to be improving since he moved into Adam's and Beth's house. By the time the summer warmth came, the Rikofians had shed most of their air of sadness. Though it was obvious that they still regretted the loss of their home island, their natural buoyancy began to assert itself.

This lightness of spirit helped to modify the Halcyon islanders' stolidity and to bring about a sunnier atmosphere. And, without noticing it, the islanders stopped referring to the incomers as a separate group; they became Mua and Otipo, Tamaru and Aola and the rest, all known individually by name and seen every day, living and working alongside Halcyon folk.

Halcyon had recovered from the first body-blow. The second was soon to come.

On a day in early summer, Thomas saw the mauled remains of a rabbit lying near an entrance to a burrow. He supposed a dog must have caught it, and thought nothing of the sight. Then children collecting seabirds' eggs and chicks began to find ledges strewn with empty shells or partly-eaten bodies. Dan Wilde, lifting early potatoes, noticed that tubers had been nibbled, and called Adam; and out of a corner of his eye Adam saw a small brown shape scuttling along the drystone wall of the vegetable plot.

A minute later, the Wildes' dog Match was barking and yelping excitedly, and trying to thrust his muzzle between the stones. Two or three more shapes appeared. Match pounced on one of them, and a dying squeal came from his victim. Dan got it from him with some difficulty. It was a furry creature a few inches long, with gray-brown coat and pale belly, bright eyes and long scaly tail. Dan hadn't seen one before, but he knew what it was.

Match was back at the wall immediately. Dan pulled out a couple of stones, uncovering a nest with half a dozen small pink naked creatures in it. The dog fell upon the nest, and Dan picked up his spade and clouted a big adult rat as it ran away. He and Adam looked at each other grimly.

'They've come,' Adam said. 'I was afraid they would.'

Some at least of Charlie Herrick's little friends had got together. Now their offspring were finding the conditions on the island to their liking, and multiplying at the rate of a generation every few weeks. The spectacular arithmetic of rats' breeding rates was about to be demonstrated.

Damage that summer was done mostly on the mountainside and cliffs, and in the wilder parts of the island. The rats seized eggs, devoured young seabirds on the nest, attacked wild rabbits and sometimes took over their burrows. The frail, slim island fowl, which hid in long grass and scrub and couldn't fly, having never before been threatened by any beast of prey, was one of the first victims. Rats found their way through its intricate paths and tunnels, and hunted it rapidly to extinction.

By summer's end, they were moving down toward the settlement. More and more of them invaded the vegetable patches. When the first maincrop potatoes were lifted it was plain that the damage was serious. Adam ordered a rat-hunt. All the active men and the half-dozen dogs joined in. The rats had nested in gaps in the stone walls. The dogs, barking furiously, located nest after nest, and waited ready to pounce as the stones were dragged away.

Rats that escaped the dogs were attacked by men with sharpened sticks, the Rikofians skewering them with remarkable accuracy. After a couple of hours, the battlefield was littered with small raw red carcases; no more rats could be found, and the dogs, their bloodlust aroused, were snapping and snarling at each other. Thomas, a reluctant participant in the affray, was white-faced and slightly sick.

'You were right to say we should keep the dogs, Adam,' Jacob Wilde admitted. 'We needed them today all right. Well done, lad!' He slapped Adam on the back. 'I reckon we dealt with the problem.'

'Not for long,' said Adam.

In spite of some damage, the crop was good, and enough potatoes were lifted to see Halcyon through the winter. But, as Adam had feared, the story wasn't over. The rats soon made good their losses. They ate half the apples from the trees in the Dell. And as the second winter approached, they moved into the houses and outbuildings. Food scraps left lying around were filched instantly. At night, the pattering of rat feet could be heard in every house, and sometimes a squeal as a rat was caught by dog or cat.

In midwinter William Jonas went to the stone outhouse where he kept his stores, picked up a sack of potatoes, and saw the gnawed remains of its contents fall out through a hole in the bottom. The rats had got them after all. Most of the villagers, it turned out, had suffered similar depredations.

A series of rat-hunts took place through the outhouses. But the rats had too many escape routes, and often got away. Adam called a meeting to discuss the threat.

'We've no poisons,' he said, 'and we've not had much luck yet with home-made traps. But we don't have to *help* the little brutes! Look at the stuff I found in a rat's-nest in somebody's storeplace; I won't say whose.' And he showed the islanders a collection of bits of gristle, fish skins, potato peelings, a sheep's knuckle bone, and a variety of household refuse. 'They love all this. They'll eat it or live in it or both. Tomorrow we start a tidying-up campaign!'

There was a good deal of grumbling, especially among older people who'd never seen the need for such care before. But storeplaces were made secure, food put in boxes as far as possible, scraps burned and daily inspections carried out. The campaign showed results. Many rats starved. With breeding reduced by the winter season and lack of food, the menace receded, though it wasn't the end.

Meanwhile an autumn expedition to Kingfisher had brought home a useful harvest from Charlie's garden, and the Rikofian men cornered and speared two wild goats. During this second winter since the departure of Harry and his friends, Beth gave birth to a girl, and Rebecca Wilde, though over forty, bore a healthy boy. One new Rikofian was born.

In spring, as always, the seabirds came again. There was food, the rats seemed under control, and the people were at peace with each other. Human life, precarious but clinging tightly to the rock that gave it reluctant support, had survived on Halcyon.

Chapter 15

On a clear blue day in spring, after Meeting, Dan took Molly across the upland, past the vegetable plots, and round toward the Dell, where the apple trees were in blossom. On the grass between the trees he turned to her to wrestle. Strong as Molly was, Dan had grown stronger, and unless she could catch him off balance as she had done once before he was bound to defeat her.

Soon she realized that that was not his aim. He sought body contact as they struggled; kissed her and fought with her at the same time. Molly was aware of his desire when he pressed against her. She didn't resent it, nor did she resist when he put his hands inside her clothing. She was still not excited by Dan as an individual, but there was something slow and deep inside her that said the time had arrived, as it did for every beast and bird on Halcyon. If Dan had persisted, her response might have come, like a great wave turning over; but Dan wasn't expecting it, wasn't ready for it, would probably have been overwhelmed by it. He took off the pressure and resumed wrestling, trying now to win. Molly let him. Afterwards, still fully clothed, they got up from the ground and went on their way.

'I can build a house, Moll,' Dan said after a while. 'We got enough timber. My dad and my uncle both have some put by.'

'Oh?' said Molly, cool now and knowing what was coming.

'And they'd help me build. My dad thinks it's time I settled.'

'You're young, Dan.'

'I'm nineteen now, and you're eighteen. It's not all that young. I count as a man these days. It's right I should be wed.'

Molly said nothing.

'So when will it be, Moll? When'll we be married?'

'I ain't thought about it,' said Molly.

'Well, it's time you did. My dad's spoken to your dad. Your dad would have given a dowry — a couple of sheep and some blankets — but my dad said there was no need, the Wildes is better off than the Reeveses, we got lots of sheep.'

'I don't know that I want to be married, yet.'

'Don't be daft, Moll. There's nine or ten girls on this island and I'm the only lad, except Thomas. I could have any one of them, but it's you I've chosen. Your dad'll have something to say if you don't have me.'

'I shan't let my dad decide for me.'

'Trouble is, Moll,' said Dan without rancour, 'you fancy Otipo, even now. Don't you?'

'That's right, Dan,' said Molly, surprised by this insight. 'How did you know?'

'I'm not as slow as you think. Well, I don't mind you fancying him, Moll. But fancying a lad ain't everything. Fancy don't own no sheep. And when it comes to the point, you're my girl, see? We was meant for each other since we was little, and I'll have you in the end.'

'We'll see,' said Molly.

Adam and Beth were at Molly's house, with the Reeves family and Aola, when she got home. Dick Reeves had been waiting for her.

'Well, Molly girl,' he said, 'have you something to tell us?'

'Dan asked me,' Molly said. 'And wanted me to fix a date.'

'And what did you say?'

'I said I'd think about it.'

Dick Reeves frowned. Hester looked uneasily at him.

'Well,' she said, defending Molly, 'it don't do to rush things.'

'She ought to know her mind by now,' said Dick. 'She always knew Dan'd want to wed her some day. This can't have come as no surprise.'

'Maybe it didn't,' said Molly. 'But he never actually asked me before. So I didn't consider it. Now I have to.'

'Hoity-toity!' said Dick. 'I don't know what things is coming to. Halcyon lasses didn't behave like this in *my* young days. Well, I'm telling you straight, Molly Reeves, I don't want you turning up your nose at a good lad like Dan!'

'I ain't turning up my nose at anyone,' said Molly. 'I'm taking my time, that's all!'

'Seems to me,' said Thomas, 'that it don't much matter what you do on Halcyon, it won't make no difference. You'll just live out your life in ignorance, same as everyone else. I been reading in Charlie's books about the outside world. There's great cities with thousands of people, and there's roads and rivers, and there's trade, and there's more things grown and made than you've ever heard of, and there's music and sports and travel and paintings, and places where people go to spend their whole lives just learning. And here we are, stuck on this tiny island. What do we know about life?'

'We know *some* things,' said Adam mildly. 'We're alive here, the same as anywhere else.'

'You call it being alive?' Thomas said. 'I wouldn't stay here if I had a chance to go anywhere else. And maybe I *will* have a chance. It must be about time a ship came. How long is it since the last one?'

'That was the *Arabella*,' said Dick. 'Eight years ago, or maybe nine, I lose count.'

'The truth is,' said Adam, 'we may never see another ship. What with the whalers going farther south, now that there's hardly any whales left in these latitudes, and what with the steamers that don't need the trade winds and never come near here, there's no reason I can think of why any ship should ever call again.'

'And if that's how it is, well and good!' said Dick. 'Let's get back to living in peace, say I.'

'All the same,' said Hester Reeves, 'there *could* be a ship one of these days. Who knows?'

That was the moment at which the Meeting-House bell began to ring. Loudly, excitedly, again and again and again.

Jemmy Wilde was helping Luke to ring the bell, leaping at the rope, tugging wildly, and shouting all the time at the top of his shrill voice.

'Sail-oh! Sail-oh!'

Islanders poured from their homes, running first for the Lookout. And from there it could be seen: a high handsome two-masted schooner, fore-and-aft rigged, no more than three or four miles from the island, and moving with stately beauty in an easy breeze.

The boat-crew hurried down to the landing-place. A dozen pairs of hands dragged the new boat, *Fulmar*, to the beach, and pushed her out through the surf.

The last ship to pass Halcyon had contemptuously dipped its ensign and sailed on. But this schooner came abreast of the landing-place and hove to, a mile from shore. The island boat drew alongside. Lines were thrown and *Fulmar* made fast.

Adam led the way up a swinging rope-ladder. On the deck, waiting beside the captain with massive hand outstretched, was Charlie Herrick.

'We brought you one or two things that might be useful,' he said.

On the deck were crates, bales, barrels, stacks of timber. 'And there's more in the hold,' said Charlie.

'Where's all this from?' Adam asked, astonished. 'We don't have money to pay for it. Is someone giving us it?'

'Nobody ain't giving no one nothing,' said Charlie. 'And you do have money, or at least you did. I took the liberty of spending it for you, seeing you wasn't there to spend it yourselves. And now, leave your questions till later while we get all this ashore.'

Two boats were lowered from the ship's side and began a series of trips. They carried timber, tools, nails and screws, fishing gear, sailcloth, rope, glass, bales of material, guns and powder and shot . . . the tally seemed endless. One boat on one of its trips was a-squawk with poultry; another brought ashore pigs and rabbits. At the end of the day, a new twenty-foot clinker-built launch carried Charlie and Captain Hammond to the landing-place, on their way to supper with Beth and Adam in the Reader's house.

'The launch is yours, too,' Charlie remarked casually as he stepped ashore.

Charlie had asked that Molly and Thomas, Otipo and Mua should all join the supper party. 'I want a chance to talk to my old friends,' he said as they sat down.

'Aren't you here for long, Charlie?' Adam asked.

'No. Well, not on Halcyon. It's not like London, but it's still too busy for Charlie Herrick. I aim to go back to Kingfisher and enjoy my peace and quiet again.'

'And what became of Harry and Bob and the others?'

'Ah, well,' said Charlie. 'They was asking for trouble, wasn't they, trying to continue the old old story? They got it, I'm afraid. Couple of days out from Halcyon, there was the worst storm I ever seen, worse than rounding Cape Horn, waves fifty foot high. It finished *Seamew*. We saw her swamped, not a stone's throw away. There was nothing we could do about it. Nobody stood a chance.'

'Was Harry at the helm?' Adam asked.

'Oh no. Harry was smart. He knew *Shearwater* was the better boat. He made sure he was in that: him and Bob and me and my instruments and Joseph Kane's chest. And Alec Campbell and Len was in *Shearwater*, too. So there was us five left. The sea calmed down soon after. But a day or two later Harry quarrelled with Bob. Oh, he was a violent man, that Bob. Stabbed Harry and tipped him overboard.'

'And what happened to Harry then?'

'Well, there's lots of sharks in them seas, you know, and they soon smells blood . . .'

'All right,' said Thomas hastily. 'And the others?'

'They had me set a course for Rikofia first. The way the *Delivery* went, but in the opposite direction. There ain't much left of Rikofia, I'm afraid, after the volcano blew its top, and we didn't find anyone alive. And by the time we got there we'd all had enough of Bob. We made a suggestion to him. We thought he might like to be landed there with a fair share of supplies and see how he got on. He didn't much care for the idea at first, but his friends persuaded him, as you might say.'

Charlie grinned.

'That left you and Alec and Len, then, didn't it, Charlie?'

'That's right. Well, the other two and me became friends, being all in the same boat as you might say. We wondered whether to turn back for Halcyon, but the winds was against us, so we decided to make for England. It wasn't much fun, though. We was three weeks at sea after Rikofia, and running short of everything, when we was picked up by a Royal Navy frigate and carried into Portsmouth. And we had some explaining to do, I can tell you, three men and a fortune.'

Charlie grinned again, reminiscently.

'Len and Alec got a chance to decamp soon after we landed, and they took it,' he said. 'We ain't likely to see *them* again. Thought they was dropping me in the dirt, they did. But Charlie knows a thing or two. Charlie knows when you can play it straight and square and not be the loser. That chest was handed over to the Crown, and everything in it. And what I've brought you today is the reward, but I thought you might like to have it in goods rather than money.'

'Charlie, you're a marvel,' said Adam. 'You're a great survivor.'

'Aye, I reckon I am,' said Charlie with satisfaction. 'And by the way, Adam, I don't know if you seen it among the stuff we landed today, but I brought you something else I thought you might need. I hope I'm wrong, but I wasn't taking no chances. It's a good stock of rat poison.'

'You were all too right, Charlie,' said Adam.

'I'm sorry about the rats. I'd never have let them out myself. Once you've got rats you can't get rid of them, any more than you can get rid of sin. All you can do is live with them and try to keep them down.'

'You're a smart man, Charlie Herrick,' said Captain Hammond. 'I wish I could sign you on. There's a first mate's berth for you any time you like.'

'No, no, I finished with the sea. It's me old enemy. I don't want to do no more than look at it, ever again.'

'Maybe you could sign *me* on, Captain?' said Thomas.

'You?' The captain looked Thomas up and down. 'And what would *you* do on my ship?'

'I just want to earn my passage,' Thomas said. 'I have to see something outside Halcyon. I'm hungry for knowing about the world. I might come back later, but just for now Halcyon hasn't got what I need.'

'Ah, well,' Captain Hammond said. 'Charlie thought of that as well. He thinks of everything. We have room for a few passengers. If there are others here who've had enough, we'll take them to civilization with us.'

'Abby'll come, for one,' said Thomas, delighted.

'But you won't find many more,' said Adam.

'Not yourself, for instance?' the captain asked.

'No, sir, not me. The day I became Reader, I took this island as I took a wife, and that's for the rest of my time.'

'It's no use arguing with *him*,' said Charlie. He turned to Otipo.

'Well, Teepo me old friend, how's *your* people getting on?'

'You must ask the chief,' said Otipo, pointing at Mua.

'Well, as you see, we are still here,' said Mua. 'We keep our own customs. But whether the two peoples will come together or stay apart, I don't know. I shan't give any ruling. We shall just see what happens. That's right, isn't it, Adam?'

'That's right,' said Adam. 'Seems fair enough to me.'

Mua was smiling.

'For himself, Otipo would prefer to mix,' she said. 'He likes an island girl better than any of ours.'

Otipo looked aside, embarrassed.

'You mean . . ?' Molly began.

'It's our Moll he likes, isn't it?' said Thomas. 'But there's competition. Dan's asked for her already.'

'What does Molly think about it?' Charlie inquired.

Molly stood up. Suddenly she felt strong and sure of herself, as strong and sure as she'd felt on the cliff face, knowing she couldn't fall. She wasn't going to fall now. She was big healthy capable Molly Reeves, alive to her fingertips, and independent. She still fancied Otipo, but Dan was steadfast and had all those sheep. It was a matter for proper consideration.

'I like them both,' she said. 'I ain't made my mind up. I'll maybe take one of them, if I feel like it. Nobody's going to push me. I might know my mind tomorrow, or next week, or next year, I'm not saying. I'll go down the Dell with either of them, and I'll decide when I'm good and ready, and that's all I have to say, thank you very much.'

There was a startled silence. Mua smiled again; then, uncertainly, so did Otipo.

'Well!' said Charlie. 'Ain't nobody going to quote the Teaching?'

'I ain't interested in the Teaching!' snapped Molly. 'Twasn't the Teaching that got us through them last two winters, was it? It was sticking together and meaning to live, that's what it was. Well, I'm still meaning to live, the best way I can, and I'll find out how for myself!'

No one had anything to say to that. After a pause Adam changed the subject.

'Cap'n Hammond,' he said, 'you brought us a great many things today. I'll give you something to take away with you. I've asked my council, and they say I can. It's no more use to us, but maybe it ought to be where people can see it.'

'Deliverer help us!' gasped Thomas. 'He's giving away the Book!'

'Well done,' said Charlie. 'You don't need it now, nor the Deliverer neither. Like Molly says, you've delivered yourselves. And, life on Halcyon being what it is, I dare say you'll have to do it again before you've finished.'

'I dare say we will,' said Adam.